Sin

A Collection of Paranormal Erotica by

Leigh Ellwood

Sinful Surprises copyright 2006-2012 by Kathryn Lively

All rights reserved under the International and Pan-American Copyright Conventions. No part of this book may be reproduced or transmitted in any form or by any means, electronic or mechanical, including photocopying, recording, or by any information storage and retrieval system, without permission in writing from the publisher.

This is a work of fiction. Names, places, characters and incidents are either the product of the author's imagination or are used fictitiously, and any resemblance to any actual persons, living or dead, organizations, events or locales is entirely coincidental.

ISBN: 978-1477622155
Cover art design by Amanda Kelsey
First DLP Edition – June, 2012

10 9 8 7 6 5 4 3 2 1

Warning: the unauthorized reproduction or distribution of this copyrighted work is illegal. Criminal copyright infringement, including infringement without monetary gain, is investigated by the FBI and is punishable by up to 5 years in prison and a fine of $250,000.

Author's Note

The following stories have been made available individually in digital format. This is the first time they have been published in trade paperback format.

Leading Lady

Chapter One

Dina stared at the black-and-white likeness of her younger self and poised a thick-tipped pen over the smooth curve of her photographed bare neck. "Hello, darling," she greeted the wide-eyed man standing before her. "This is for whom, now?"

He couldn't have been more than twenty-five. Thick, dirty blond hair hung in clumps over one brow. A large button covering one breast of his Metallica T-shirt informed the world that his phaser was always set for "stunning." Dina imagined the collective sigh of relief settling around the room from any female conventioneers having seen that button.

"Gr-Gregory," he croaked.

"Gregory. Thank you, Gregory." The syllables rolled off her tongue with seductive ease; she trilled the first *R* with her trademark purr, the same throaty growl that had sent thousands of Gregorys into euphoric wet dreams over the years. It was the satisfied deep trill that had broken color barriers on television and had proved to a network skittish over the ratings in backwater Alabama that, yes, a black woman had the talent and sex appeal to attract a mass audience. That seductive power, coupled with the skimpy costumes and lustrous fake topknot of flowing dark hair, garnered Dina twice the fan mail of her white costars.

Not to mention all the prime gigs at cons around the world, and the prime fans -- top billing over movie actors, even. This Gregory, looking so young, had to be a recent admirer as opposed to one of the legion of first-generation faithful, a fan who had come to know *Mission: Jupiter* through endless reruns on cable or the recent DVD releases of the popular 1970s science fiction series.

Either way, Dina thought, *he's here, and so am I.* He had forked over his ten bucks admission fee and the five-dollar charge for the glossy photo her assistant distributed from the stack at the next table. His presence paid for at least one drink she had enjoyed last night at the hotel bar.

He was cute, too. Maybe he'd be good for more than his money.

Dina smiled to herself and crossed her legs tighter to counter the sudden desire flooding her pussy, rustling the star field print tablecloth in the process.

"I-I just wanted you to know," Gregory continued as Dina scribbled a random platitude and a loopy signature on the photograph, "that you're my favorite character on *MJ*."

"Thank you, Gregory. That's so sweet of you to say." That's what everybody called *Mission: Jupiter* these days. *Star Trek* was referred to as either *Trek Classic*, *TNG*, or *DS9*, depending on the proper incarnation, and other popular sci-fi favorites suffered similar abbreviation. Dina disliked it; *MJ* sounded more like an illegal sex act performed in an alley behind a liquor store.

She glanced at the photograph, giving it one final inspection. It was a stock publicity photo of her twenty-five-year-old self attired in her incredibly sexist *Mission: Jupiter* uniform. She had to laugh every time she saw the action pose of Lieutenant Mayda Moran, wearing a formfitting mini dress and white go-go boots with hoop earrings, pointing a phaser at the camera like she meant business. The men on the show had worn jumpsuits suitable for NASA; the women looked like waitresses at a strip club.

Of course, she was the favorite character of all the Gregorys. Dina studied the photo. *Look at the tits on that phaser-wielding wench!* This was a woman who had defied gravity and laws of physics merely by slinking past fellow officers along the corridors of the *USS Jupiter* every Monday night for five years. Never mind that Mayda had been the only officer on the ship capable of rubbing two brain cells together in order to formulate plans to defeat the evil Narciscans, *look at those tits*. These were the show's biggest stars, pun intended. That's what Gregory was addressing as he complimented her, Dina knew.

She sat up straight. The two biggest stars of *Mission: Jupiter* continued to defy gravity well into Dina's forties, without the aid of plastic surgery, thank you very much. The quest to remain young for the cameras by way of a sadistic exercise and diet regimen had seen to that, for all the good it did. The body remained fit, the skin as smooth and flawlessly cocoa as ever, but producers saw only a stock character from a campy sci-fi TV show when it came time to cast for serious dramas. To think, with the door open wider for African American actresses now, she could find better roles outside the occasional guest-starring bit on a weekly series.

Thanks for screwing my big-time movie career, chick. She mock scowled at the young girl in the picture and planted a pouty kiss on her rump to the collective gasp of fans clustered around her table. She then slid the photo across the table into Gregory's trembling fingers. There was no mistaking the delight on the young man's face; he checked the Internet, Dina was certain. He knew the code.

"Wow. Thanks, Mayda," Gregory said, and floated away. Dina sighed. It used to bother her to be referred to by her character's name, but when opportunities for work had dried up, Dina had eventually come to accept her alter ego with the rising demand for her appearance at science-fiction conventions. Mayda was a part of her now, a part she had quickly come to appreciate for its fringe benefits despite her occasional grousing. At the very least, none of her white female costars from the show had been able to break free from the *Mission Jupiter* curse to find success in television again, and Dina rarely saw them at cons.

She watched Gregory, one possible benefit of the con circuit, stride confidently to a remote corner of the hotel ballroom, and then turn expectantly back toward her table. He knew now that the legend was true…that a lipstick mark on an autographed Dina Joseph was a special, coveted treasure. He was in contention with other lucky conventioneers to fuck Mayda Moran herself. He held the proof in his hands like a golden ticket to the chocolate factory.

Gregory had a deliciously tight ass encased in black jeans, and judging from the pronounced bulge in the front, he definitely advertised that he was more than just fringe. Perhaps he did pack impressive heat, as his button advertised. Dina smiled at him; there was that pulsing sensation that engorged her pussy lips. Yes, she definitely appreciated these opportunities.

"Jenna, you know the drill." She craned her neck as she quietly addressed Jenna McCoy, her personal assistant. "Screen test, money shot."

Jenna smirked and fished through her bulky shoulder sack for a digital camera. "Six we nix?"

"Seven is heaven," Dina confirmed. "Eight, great, and nine is *divine.*" The two women giggled over the puzzled look on the next fan's face.

Dina then watched Jenna approach Gregory and, after viewing a few silent words and restrained hand gestures, smiled to see the young man willingly follow the young black woman with the dark ponytail behind a blue cloth partition. There, Gregory would "audition" by letting down his pants and allowing Jenna to take a picture for Dina to later peruse. *Six we nix.* A six-inch cock or less was an automatic reject...but seven or more was a definite casting, and Gregory would get the part provided he wasn't surpassed by another. Dina had seen enough cock in her day to discern size for herself, no tape measure was necessary.

She returned to her audience. She wondered how many of the other men snaked around the convention space in the various autograph lines would be willing to put themselves through the rigorous audition expected of a lipstick-printed fan?

The autograph session dragged, and when three o'clock mercifully arrived, Dina was down to her last original nicety. Her hand cramped from signing, and her pussy ached for want of a young stud's attention. The myths of sci-fi conventions were just that -- there was nary a pocket protector or taped-up pair of horn-rims to be seen in this crowd. Dina saw handsome young men in T-shirts advertising various fandoms, curvy women in skimpy character dress, and older fans weathering age quite well. A few decades out of the sun, watching the same *Mission: Jupiter* episodes over and again, was clearly good for the skin.

Despite the collective musk of hormones settling in the room, however, this con proved somewhat of a disappointment compared to others. She had marked only three other fans since Gregory. Surprisingly, all four fell short of the prerequisite. Phasers had apparently been set for *dud* tonight. *Sorry, boys,* Dina thought as she bid the last fan farewell, *you must be so big to ride.*

Jenna helped her close up shop and counted the till. "Not a bad haul," the assistant remarked, fanning a wad of bills into a metal money box. She counted out the required ten percent to cover the con's share and snapped the lid shut.

"Moneywise, anyway," Dina grumbled.

"Sorry, hon." Jenna pouted. "I blame these new jeans the kids are wearing. They wrinkle weird. False advertising."

"Yeah, and here I used to think false advertising meant me endorsing a product on TV that I never used." She laughed. It hurt, for she was probably going to bed alone tonight. Jenna might have sufficed -- the girl was always willing -- but she'd really wanted a cock.

"Well, you'll score at next month's New Jersey gig, I just know it. We'll need to order more Mayda pictures for that too," Jenna said. "We should probably get rid of those other ones; I don't know why you keep them, Dee. Nobody ever buys them."

"I know." Dina sighed at the stack of publicity shots Jenna placed into an accordion folder. The photos depicted her in regal dress for her only major film role, an epic that had played to empty movie houses and was never released on DVD. Dina had no way to sell copies if people didn't even remember the film.

"I didn't even go see it," she told Jenna. "About a month of box office, shown on network television once. Now it's locked in an airless vault with other turkeys."

"Was it that bad? The costume is gorgeous. Looks like a big-budget flick."

"Not really, more a labor of love sort of thing for this guy I was seeing. He started out as head writer on *Mission: Jupiter* before breaking into film. He knew I always wanted to play a queen, so he wrote the script for me." Dina lifted her chin. A sad smile touched her face as she thought of Alan Widmark. Of all her lovers, he was the only one with whom she would have considered having a long-term relationship or, dare she suggest it in a time where interracial relationships were eyed with scrutiny, marriage. She might have pursued it, too, had he not died shortly after the film was released. When Dina learned of the car accident, occurring after Alan had left her house, she couldn't bring herself to see the film. The tragedy had done little to boost box office or inspire sympathy raves. The film simply died with its director.

"I was always afraid I'd jinx my career if I ever saw myself on-screen," she told Jenna instead. It was the truth, to an extent, but her life with Alan was her own. "I never watched an episode of *Mission: Jupiter*, either. Figured if I watched myself perform, I'd never work again. Guess I should've done the opposite, huh?"

Jenna handed her a DVD set of the show's first season. "Never too late. Pop in a disc, maybe Spielberg will call."

Yeah, like I have no big plans tonight. Dina waved away the package with a smirk. She *didn't* have plans, thanks to false advertising. "Please, girl. I haven't worked for years outside a con, so I wouldn't know what to do anymore. And I won't degrade myself by participating in one of those reality shows that feature other one-trick ponies, either." This was a long-suggested idea she knew Jenna would revisit. Best to head her off at the pass.

"It's a nice paycheck," Jenna sang, "and it might bring in offers of legitimate work. It has for other actors."

"Yeah, it got them other reality shows. It's not worth the hassle of living in a tricked-up mansion listening to a bunch of other has-beens spout their retro catchphrases. Forget it." Dina stood and arched her back, working out the kinks. The only reality she wanted to face was a warm tub and a soft bed, seeing as how the added bonus of a hard body to join her in both wasn't likely. "Let's get out of here."

"Ms. Joseph?"

Dina almost didn't turn her head; few people addressed her by her real name. Even her shrink called her Mayda.

When she snapped around to see the two gorgeous men standing before her dismantled station, she knew instantly that she wouldn't have minded playing doctor with either of them. Or both.

Each was the photo-negative image of the other -- porcelain white and dark olive, almost Mediterranean -- and both sported soft brown eyes and hair cropped behind pointed ears. That narrowed their possible fandom preference to six shows. *Mission: Jupiter* had its share of characters with pointed ears and eyebrows, webbed feet and hands, and whatever other physical anomalies the writers concocted while drinking.

The olive-skinned one had blond hair; his otherworldly look well suited the convention. Dina wondered if the man wore makeup to enhance his shading. He sported an Eisenhower jacket and black pants that nicely accentuated his muscled thighs and front bulge. Not a wrinkle to be seen. A leather strap around one shoulder indicated he had a scabbard behind his back; a sword handle protruded from behind one shoulder.

Nice.

The dark-haired one was definitely paler by comparison, save for the piercing water blue eyes, and was dressed entirely in white. The uniform and gilded insignia resembled nothing from any TV show she had seen, but there were a number of European TV fandoms represented here. He could be representative of any of them, for all she knew. Dina was already a fan of his equally impressive groin.

Please, let one of them be divine. "Yes, I am Dina Joseph," she said. It felt strange to say that. She saw herself more as Mayda Moran than her real self. The thought to offer a free autograph faded quickly. Despite the obvious costume, she got the feeling these men were not *Mission: Jupiter* fans. "How can I help you?"

The two men looked knowingly at each other before the blond spoke again. "I am Kray, and this is my, er, partner, Lane. As you can see, neither of us have signed photos bearing lipstick markings." He winked. "Nevertheless, we have noticed you are still alone..."

Dina wanted to roll her eyes at this. *Thanks.*

"...and we are hoping this will not prevent us from, ah, an *audition*," Kray finished.

"I see." Dina caught a peripheral glance of Jenna, whose eyes were practically popping from her sockets. The younger woman was a better judge of size than she when looking at *clothed* men. The night might end well for her, after all. "Well," she said slyly, "certainly I'm not above bending the rules. A kissed photo isn't necessarily the only invitation I offer."

"There is one catch, Ms. Joseph," the dark-haired universal soldier broke in. "We would like to audition as a pair."

"Meaning?" Dina thought she might orgasm at the husky tone of his voice.

"Meaning," the blond rejoined, "if we both pass, we both play. And, if we may be so bold" -- his hand flipped upward to reveal some snapshots pinched between his fingers -- "we've taken the liberty of performing our own screen test for your consideration."

"Well..." Dina was grateful for her training. On the outside she regarded the proposal coolly, yet within her, she battled every nerve that fought to splay wide her legs right there on the table. The photos Kray handed her revealed two cocks, impressive even in their flaccid states. Her pussy felt ready to melt. She couldn't remember the last time she had enjoyed a *divine* rod. Actually, she could. Alan, despite having been twice Dina's age, sported a nine-inch cock and knew how to use it. Lord, but she missed that man.

Here, though, she was being offered two in the preferred size range and a hotel key card held by the dark-haired one. Her kind of sweeps week.

"Shall we say, seven?" Kray asked.

She took the card. "We shall." Now she couldn't decide if seven or nine was her favorite number.

Chapter Two

"This won't work."

Kray looked up from the row of winking candles arranged on the bureau. The overhead lights were dimmed, soft music wafted from the small bedside radio, and room-service champagne chilled in a bucket stand by the bed. A scene for seduction was set as best as the two could arrange it.

Everything seemed workable to Kray, save for the combination of burning vanilla and lavender that stung his nostrils. He had forgotten how noxious the scents were to him, yet this was what Dina Joseph liked, according to the information they had on her. For this to work, everything had to go as planned, and that meant for Kray to control his olfactory discomfort and for Lane to not act so skeptical.

"This won't work," Lane said again.

"We'll have to suck up the odor." Kray nodded to the candles. "It's a nice night out. Maybe if we open the balcony doors, it won't bother us as much."

"I don't mean the candles, Kray, I mean this whole thing. This. *Us*." Lane, clad only in a pair of jogging shorts, paced their hotel room, his tension evident in his gait. "I don't think we can pull this off. She's going to see right through us."

"She won't. She's used to meeting up with odd people at these conventions. Whatever quirks that slip past, she'll attribute to some kind of science-fiction fanaticism she thinks we're harboring." Kray perched on one corner of the bed and tracked Lane's every movement. Lane was beautifully sculpted, from his strong arms to his taut, bare legs. The obvious anxiety Lane exuded overrode the discomfort from the candles' too-sweet aroma. Kray felt suddenly dizzy and wobbled.

"Lane." Kray scooted farther onto the mattress and gestured the fairer man to sit between his legs. He ground his fingers into Lane's shoulders to undo the knots bunched in the other man's muscles. Lane was always a delight to touch. He felt his cock stir between them. It had been a while since they had made love, and Kray felt well the effects of withdrawal. The scent of Lane so close taunted him. It was all he could do to keep from thrashing Lane back onto the mattress and straddling his gorgeous body. Two days since Kray last felt Lane's delightful tongue teasing his erect shaft and puckered hole...two days too long.

Patience, Kray reminded himself. They had to save something for Dina.

"Dina is beautiful." Lane's voice was soft.

"So are you." He brushed a kiss into Lane's hair.

"I can only hope I'm worthy of her, and that I'll please her."

"You are, and you will. And she will love you. Everything is going to be fine," Kray assured Lane. "By morning, Dina will be crazy for us and willing to leave this nothing of a life behind her."

"By morning, we'll be in prison after she has us arrested or committed." Lane caught Kray's hand as it slid down his shoulder. "She's a smart woman. What makes you think she'll believe us?"

"Faith, my love. She is the one for us." Kray leaned forward and kissed the bend in Lane's neck.

"How do we explain these?" Lane tapped at a pointed ear. "How do we explain they don't come off when she asks us to remove them?"

"Eccentricity." Kray let Lane guide his hand across Lane's broad chest. He rolled a toughened nipple between his thumb and forefinger, and was satisfied as Lane relaxed. "We're science-fiction fans. We want to ravish the luscious Mayda Moran while dressed as those Narciscan characters on her old TV show." That was the agreed-upon cover, the fetish excuse they planned to deliver should Dina question the ears. "I'm sure others have made similar concessions with her, some even stranger than pointed ears."

"We're *not* science-fiction fans. We're *elves*," Lane said, though the edge in his voice softened significantly as Kray's hand found the soft sac between his legs and squeezed. "She's not going to believe we're from an alternate reality, much less that we're not human, that *I'm* not, anyway. You're half-human, at least."

"I don't look it, though. Don't presume to know what's going to happen, Lane. You might be surprised with how well our plan is executed."

"She finds out these ears are real, we'll be executed when she dies of fright." Lane's voice was heavy. "They'll think we killed her."

Kray nipped at Lane's earlobe. "Such delicious ears, too. Dina will love them as much as I do. She'll be fine." Lane appeared to fight his caresses, but Kray could feel his partner continuing to succumb.

"Weren't the Narciscans the villains on that show?" Lane asked. "Why would any of them want to sleep with an officer of the *Jupiter*?"

"We can fill in plot holes later, love." Kray pressed a finger to Lane's chin and forced him closer for a light kiss. "Tonight, we claim Dina Joseph as our own." Lane's worries were unfounded. By the time they were through with the lovely Dina, the actress would willingly take her place in the triad and take on her new role as queen of her husbands' hearts.

Lane was completely relaxed now and fell forward to straddle Kray's hips as the two men kissed. This was exactly what he had wanted to prevent, but it felt too nice to ignore any further. Kray's cock pressed against Lane, and he ached to be inside him; Lane was a sensuous, giving lover, and Kray blessed every day they were together. To have Dina finally join them would be heaven. No way would the consummate actress turn down the role of a lifetime…the role of an alternate lifeline, and a life much better than the one she currently lived.

Kray kissed Lane's throat, his collarbone, his breastbone, and continued a soft, loving trail down Lane's body. He loved the way the handsome elf stiffened with every kiss. Lane was going to love having him *and* Dina doing this…forever.

Chapter Three

What is that sound?

Dina leaned into the door until her ear barely brushed the painted wood. A wicked smile curled her lips; it wasn't too difficult to decipher the deep moaning. The divine photo-negative twins had started without her. Interesting... This was going to be *that* kind of threesome.

Dina felt her nipples tighten at the thought of Kray and Lane going at it on the other side of the door. Homoerotica was a big turn on for her; these two must truly have been fans of hers to know that. The fetish wasn't something she advertised, but no doubt news of her favorite proclivities had circulated around the sci-fi convention circuit over the years.

She wondered what they were doing. Did the dark-haired one -- Lane -- have his head between Kray's thighs, sucking his cock? Their introduction had been brief, but Dina imagined Lane was likely the more submissive of the pair. She could see a man like Kray roughly pounding his cock into that delightful pale ass and enjoying every minute of it.

Oh, yes, she *really* wanted to see that. Maybe Lane would eat her pussy while she watched.

She knocked twice, hard, and waited.

"Coming!" shouted a distinctly surprised voice.

I'll bet. Dina chuckled, but said nothing.

Muffled chaos vibrated the door, and Dina smiled as she pictured the two men hastily righting their clothes and smoothing down their hair to look presentable.

She hadn't expected either man to be nearly naked, but Dina didn't complain when Kray open the door to greet her. Over his shoulder, she could see Lane lounging on the edge of the bed, idly swinging a bare leg. Where Kray's welcoming smile evinced a natural confidence that set Dina's blood rushing to her sensitive areas, Lane's shy grin proved just as endearing.

The vertical tenting of Kray's shorts was as much a delight to behold as his smooth-planed chest. Lane was equally appealing. As Kray escorted her to sit next to him, she noticed his dark nipples appeared thick, and Dina ached to bite them. The bulge in his shorts seemed to throb as he shifted for comfort.

Thank God, she thought, thinking fleetingly of her years of training by many an acting coach. Stoic outside, volcanic within. The thought of having these two magnificent specimens fucking her simultaneously, and perhaps doing more with each other, would have made her quake had she not been able to suppress the excitement. As it was, her pussy ached to the point of explosion, and she clenched to keep her juices from soaking the sheets; she feared the slightest touch by either of them would cause her to explode.

Kray stood before her, ramrod straight, yet with a relaxed expression. How he could look so blasé impressed and frustrated Dina. Despite years of playing with groupies, the notion of sex still made her giddy.

She bit her lip as Lane rose and wrapped an arm around the other man's waist.

"Ms. Joseph, as always, you are a vision of beauty," Kray said. "Lane and I thank you for coming."

"Thank you for wanting to make me come." Dina laughed awkwardly at her lame joke, relieved neither man expressed any distaste with it. They only stared down at her with a love-struck awe that quickly unnerved her. *Was coming here a wise thing to do?* she suddenly wondered. Neither man seemed like the other young men she'd fucked over the years. These two seemed interested in more than just a casual fling.

An unbidden thought drew her gaze down to her clutch purse. Jenna had the day's till in the hotel safe, but these guys didn't know that.

"Dina, you look nervous." Kray's face straightened. "Don't be. Lane and I want this to be a night you won't forget."

She might have relaxed more if Lane concurred vocally. As it was, the fairer man only stared. The thought to conjure an excuse to leave suddenly came and went when her gaze fell to their bulges. Two cocks! Huge ones, at that, circumcised tips peeking over elastic waistbands. How could she refuse?

If they turned out to be robbers and murderers, Dina decided, hopefully they'd give her the courtesy of a few good orgasms before doing the deed. Dying would only inflate her legend.

"Oh-kay. Well, let's get right to it, shall we?" She crossed her arms and reached for the hem of her scoop-necked shirt, but Lane's hand stilled hers. The electric pulse shocked her heart.

"No," Lane whispered. "You shouldn't do that."

"Why not?" Odd. This was the part where she was supposed to be naked too.

"You don't lift a finger tonight," Kray supplied. "This night, you are to be pleasured. We will do all the work. We will undress you as you wish."

"Oh, really?" *Nice.* She was going to be pampered. This was a first for the convention circuit. Past playmates tended not to be as accommodating. Dina shook her head quickly to jar away memories of those encounters: the guy who had requested a striptease, the guy who had laughed like Jerry Lewis during a blowjob, the guy who had pestered her with *Mission: Jupiter* questions as he fucked her. She wanted to concentrate on Kray and Lane; these were the only two heavenly bodies she wanted to conquer tonight, and so far, they seemed saner than others she'd had.

If only... Dina touched her own ears and arched an eyebrow at them. "About these..." she began.

Kray ran his fingers through his hair and momentarily stopped at his pointed ears. "If you please, Ms. Joseph," he said, "it's been a fantasy of ours --"

"Say no more." Dina sighed, but kept her smile. Ears weren't as conspicuous as, say, full-body armor. Now *there* was an experience she'd just as soon forget.

Both men seemed to read her mind. Tonight, there would be no *Mission: Jupiter* trivia, nothing juvenile. As Kray and Lane sat on either side of the bed, enveloping her with their heated desire, she felt ready to come at a verbal command.

Hands caressed her, smoothing over her collarbone, shoulders, and arms. As an unseen cloud of vanilla and lavender wafted around them and numbed her senses, Dina felt a cool sensation and looked down to see her exposed dark skin, raised with goose bumps. Lane had managed to remove her skirt and panties without her moving, and Kray had undone all the buttons on her blouse and was now unhooking her bra. Sometime during their ministrations, their shorts had disappeared as well. How had that happened so quickly?

Soon her breasts were free, vulnerable to their touch. Each man stroked a breast with amorous synchronicity, using roughened thumbs to circle her mocha nipples, which immediately stood to attention. Dina felt the pleasured sensation shoot straight to her pussy. She needed a cock inside her now, and judging from how much thicker the ones on either side of her had become in the last few seconds, she knew Kray and Lane had to share her thoughts.

"Soon," Kray whispered in her ear. "Let us pleasure you first..."

"Dina."

"What's that?" Kray asked.

She looked into his eyes and felt a sudden pang of anxiety. No lust raged in those deep brown eyes as she had expected. What she saw seemed...different, serious. Yet, somewhat familiar too. Dina might have felt uneasy had not Lane dissolved her reserve with a few well-timed kisses on her bare shoulder.

"Call me Dina," she said, not necessarily to Kray. "I sensed you were about to call me Ms. Joseph again." She squirmed when Kray's hand pried her legs apart. "I think we're beyond formalities. Don't call me Ms. Joseph, or Mayda." Mayda had been good to her at these shows, but Dina wanted her to have none of this. "Call me Dina."

"Of course," Kray said, "Dina."

Chapter Four

Dina. *Beloved.*

How wonderful to say that name again. How familiar it felt on his tongue after so many years of self-imposed silence. To have said her name in the past evoked only sadness and regret for what might have been. Tonight, however, signaled a new beginning for Kray, with the two most important people in his life. All the wrongs of the past decades would be reversed. Only tonight, and every night thereafter, mattered.

Kray tucked his knees underneath him and crept up the mattress behind Dina, easing her on her back. "Relax," he whispered as he stretched Dina's lithe yet suddenly tense body. She was beautiful, her skin smooth like chocolate cream, belying her true age. He couldn't wait to explore every inch of her and, watching Lane's face split into a wide grin as Dina's legs parted, looked forward as well to his partner's first experience with a woman.

Dina's pussy was as smooth as the rest of her body...ripe and delicious. Kray could see her labia twitch as Lane shouldered his way between her thighs. Gently, Kray smoothed a hand to one breast, palmed her nipple, and delighted as it brushed his skin. Her response to their touch was as he hoped -- giddy and expectant, feelings to soon give way to thrashing pleasure.

She shifted in his lap; his erection pressed into one of her shoulder blades. "Dina, please," he said, and eased her up slightly to free his cock. Pivoting toward her, he grasped his shaft at the base and aimed it for her mouth. Oh, how he ached for her touch.

"Dina, I know we said earlier we would do what you choose, but I've waited so long for this and I was hoping..."

To his relief, she didn't protest.

Dina curled her lips outward and pursed them around the bulging head of his cock. Kray thought he'd go mad when the tip of her tongue swiped at the precum bubbling on the slit. Slowly, seductively, Dina applied a suction that saw Kray's cock disappear, centimeter by centimeter, into her.

So good.

He wanted to close his eyes and savor the moment, but the sight of Lane buried between Dina's thighs was too stimulating to ignore. Lane seemed to have her entire pussy in his mouth, given the way his upper lip was clamped over her mound. His eyes closed and head wavering back and forth, Lane looked lost in his own world as he ate Dina, a world he'd be loath to depart, if Kray could correctly interpret Lane's enthusiasm.

Lane had enjoyed few partners in his time, all male, yet Kray knew the younger man was looking forward to forming this mixed triad. He had to wonder, though, how Lane was eating Dina's pussy. Did his tongue lap at her swollen lips with broad strokes as his mouth collected her juices, or maybe Lane was tracing the edges of her slick core, teasing her with penetration before sliding up to tap on her clit? Whatever he was doing, Dina was clearly enjoying it. Kray hoped there would be enough left to enjoy once Lane was finished.

As it was, Lane was close to bringing Dina to orgasm; Kray felt it through the sudden tugging on his cock as it muffled her moans of pleasure. He bent low to caress one breast, pinching the nipple as she released his cock with a light *pop* and cried her release.

"Mmmmm," Dina groaned. Kray picked up on the satisfaction humming through Dina's body as she rode the orgasm back to earth. His fingers glided over her raised flesh, reading her desires. She had enjoyed that first explosion -- yes, there would be more -- and Kray saw that she hungered still. So she would receive, but not quite so quickly.

He had waited too long to rush this night.

* * * * *

This made up for everything -- endless years of being snubbed for awards, being asked to purr catchphrases on cue by multitudes of fans, being called Mayda during auditions. As Lane lifted his head and offered her a sticky, satisfied grin, Dina realized that if, indeed, these men turned out to be criminals, they wouldn't need blunt instruments to kill her. Death by orgasm had a much, much sweeter ring to it.

"Did you enjoy it?" Lane asked, his voice betraying the confidence evident in his smile.

"Baby." She gasped, her abdomen heaving. "That was incredible." Imagine what his cock could do; her pussy twitched in anticipation.

She looked up at Kray, curious that he hadn't moved except to fondle her breasts. His cock looked near bursting. She had loved the feel of it throbbing in her mouth and longed to taste it again. Yet, she wanted the men to switch places, too. She had to know how gifted Kray was at eating pussy, had to know how good Lane tasted...

Kray seemed to read her mind. Suddenly, he edged Lane to one side and took his place between Dina's thighs. He smoothed his fingers over her moistened pussy lips, delving one finger deep into her slit to massage her inner walls. Dina gasped at his touch as it quickened, then thickened with the addition of more fingers.

She arched her back and moaned. Kray continued to assault her pussy with his hand and tongue. He lapped at her clit as his fingers scraped inside her, massaging her G-spot. Lane snaked upward on the mattress to take a nipple hard between his teeth. Every nerve ending of that breast ignited. *Oh, God, no need to take me to Heaven. I'm already there.*

Lane pulled at the nipple, then let it slip through his front teeth. "You like that?"

"Yes." Dina followed his gaze down the landscape of her body and stopped at Kray's face buried in her pussy. His technique was slower, yet equally sensuous.

"He is so beautiful," Lane said. She noted a catch in the man's voice.

"He is," she replied softly.

"I love watching him do that to you."

I love him doing it. Was that jealousy in the young man's eyes? Did he envy Kray for the opportunity to drive her to orgasm again, or did he envy her for being on the receiving end of Kray's attentions? She tried to ponder it, but the sensations building up in her pussy were too great to ignore. She lolled her head back and focused on the fire spreading up her legs.

Lane turned on his side and stroked her cheek. "What can I do for you now?" He sounded earnest.

Dina leaned closer to let him nuzzle her. "What were you two doing before I came here?" She bit back a laugh at Lane's sudden blush; she didn't want to embarrass him too much. "You said, lady's choice."

Lane looked away, but she saw a smile. *Hmmm.* Could that coy little move have been an admission of homoerotic shenanigans? If so, why act so shyly about it, Dina wondered. It was obvious to her these men had feelings for each other as well as for her. It definitely wouldn't repel her to see them in action.

She braced her arms behind her and lifted her upper body, splaying her legs farther to grant Kray better access to her pussy.

"Let me see you suck his cock," she told Lane.

* * * * *

Oh, if it were possible to love her even more…

Kray slid his hands underneath Dina's ass and eased her farther up the bed, not missing one second of attention to her mound. He continued to suckle her clit and nibble her pussy lips as he found a comfortable position below her, one that would allow Lane to devour his cock.

Lane didn't miss a beat, either. He rolled onto his back, his feet toward Dina's head, then to one side, and took Kray's thick shaft in hand. Kray looked up long enough to see Dina start to stroke Lane's erect cock; then the room blurred as Lane's lips touched his sensitive head. Dina's musk and juices, coupled with the added sensation of his balls tightening in response to Lane's ministrations, sent his body into overdrive. If he shot his load into Lane's willing mouth now, would there be enough for Dina?

Looking at her clearly enjoying the show, smiling, and cooing at them, would she care?

Kray cared, very much, for Dina's happiness and pleasure and to be clamped by her sweet vise. Yet, he enjoyed Lane's cock trapped tightly between his lips as well. It would be hell to have to ask Lane to stop.

He eased a reluctant Lane from his cock and pointed him to the nightstand. "You liked watching that, you naughty girl," he said, reveling in the low, throaty giggle that was Dina's answer. "You want to see more?"

"Baby, you bet."

He positioned his cock toward Dina's waiting, swollen core. "You want to watch me pound this cock in Lane's ass, or do you want some first?"

Her eyes widened. "You'd fuck him for me?" She looked up at an ebullient Lane as he fumbled with the foil packets in his hand. "You've done it before," she said knowingly.

"We'll do it again or not, your choice. We'll do it as we're doing you, whatever you wish. I could fuck Lane while he fucks you. That would be so sweet." It would, too, but Kray wanted his chance with her first.

"I have an idea," she said, licking her lips. "How about you take me first while I work on Lane's beautiful rod."

At the suggestion, he felt his heart lift to the ceiling.

Reluctantly, they parted long enough to allow Dina to position herself on her knees. Lane wobbled on the mattress to kneel before her, and she bowed immediately into his cock, taking him in one swallow. Grasping her buttocks and spreading them to reveal hot, waiting pussy, Kray traced the edges of her cunt with the tip of his cock before pushing into her.

"Ohhhhh." She was everything he had hoped and dreamed -- hot, tight, wet. This moment, this gentle rhythm and soft moaning accompaniment as he slid in and out of her, well made up for time lost. Kray was going to enjoy catching up with her.

He watched her suck Lane's cock, her movements jerky as he pushed into her. Her breasts shook with each thrust, and Kray longed to reach over and pluck the softened nipples back to attention. "Beautiful," he murmured, then to Lane, "Sixty-nine her."

With a smile, Lane released his hold and dived underneath her. Lying on his back, Lane presented his cock again, and Dina wasted no time reclaiming it. She moaned her approval as he paced his thrusts to Lane's assaults on her clit. Kray smiled too, with the occasional, literal, slip of the tongue as Lane lapped at the base of his cock. His pleasure heightened, so much that he almost didn't want to relinquish his position.

But this night was about making Dina happy, and she wanted to see some hot bi action. Definitely, it was a good trade-off.

"Now," he commanded and freed himself from Dina. Lane scrambled from underneath her and sheathed himself with a condom quickly before taking Kray's place. As Kray applied some lubricant to his cock, he noticed Dina appeared to be too deep in an orgasm-induced haze to register what was happening before Lane eased her on her back and drove his cock home. She then gasped at the contact. This sound, though, was nothing like the deep-throated groan Lane set free when Kray pried apart the other man's buttocks and, after teasing the eye first by inserting a finger, slowly eased his cock into the growing hole.

"Can you see?" he asked Dina, his voice huffing as he moved with Lane, like pistons in a machine, working at pleasure.

Her head lolled to one side, her face a mask of pure rapture. "No," she cried softly. "I wish I could."

"Next time." For her benefit, and Lane's, Kray bent forward and rained kissed across the other man's shoulders and back. He was rewarded by Lane clinching the proper muscles, tightening the hold.

"I'm gonna come," Kray breathed into his ear. "How do you want me to come? Do you want it in your ass? Or should I pull out and spray all over your back? He likes that," he told Dina.

"Come in my ass." Lane grunted. "Don't stop fucking me." To Dina, he said, "Let me come in your pussy. Please." He sucked in a quick breath, and Dina flicked his nipples.

"Yes," she agreed. "Fuck me hard like he's fucking you." Her voice was choppy with each hard thrust.

"Yes," Kray seethed. They reached a speed that caused skin to slap against skin and sweat to shine on Lane's back. Arms tangled and hands scratched; Kray no longer knew where Dina ended and Lane began. Their voices were a sensual chorus that rose in pitch with the simultaneous climax, Kray's being the loudest as his cock spasmed in Lane's ass. He collapsed on top of the other man, whose braced support gave away, causing them roll to one side as Dina gasped for breath.

Kray took the moment of disorientation to roll over Lane to lie near Dina's other side. Together, the men sandwiched her and caressed her to calming. Kray watched the jagged rise and fall of her breasts with deep satisfaction.

"Oh, Jesus." Dina drew the two simple words into several syllables, laughing all the while. "That...was fucking incredible."

"That," Kray rejoined, "was only the beginning."

"Oh, really?" She arched a brow at him. Lane rested his cheek against one breast, and she idly stroked the other man's rumpled mane. "Honey, I don't think I could go another round tonight. I need to have *something* left for tomorrow's Q&A appearance at the con." She chuckled. "Have to stay on my game."

"I don't mean right now, although I wouldn't mind another round," Kray said. "I meant this is the only beginning" -- he winked at Lane -- "of the rest of our lives together."

Chapter Five

Do what?

Dina sat up abruptly, trying to ignore the looks of alarm on her new lovers' faces. Loud, ringing, cuckoo noises suddenly pierced her consciousness. Certifiably insane, these two were. She should have suspected that when they wouldn't remove the pointed ears, but then she'd picked up a many a fan dressed more outrageously who didn't try to "claim her." She should have been more adamant about the ears. A more forceful refusal would have cued her to leave.

Then again, she'd have missed out on the best orgasm of her life. No-win situation. Ugh.

"Excuse me," she murmured and slid off the bed. Where were her clothes? She searched the floor around the bed and found nothing.

"Dina, have we done something to upset you?" Kray asked, concern coloring his voice. "Did you not enjoy yourself?"

She *had* enjoyed herself, immensely, but talk of forever spooked her. She'd been lucky in her life never to meet up with a truly obsessed fan of the Mark David Chapman variety, but that one word sparked an alarm within her. *Forever.* Dina shivered.

These two were cool, she had to admit. They knew the audition process, knew her favorite scents and fetishes…she should have picked up on the signals instead of listening to her aching pussy. She should have realized she might be falling into a trap.

"I'm fine," she finally managed. Where *were* her clothes? What had they done with them? She looked around the room once more, then at the two puzzled faces before her and sighed. "I-I have to go now," she said. "I'm on a panel early in the morning..."

"You don't have to go so soon," Kray said.

"We were hoping you'd stay here tonight," Lane added.

"That's sweet of you to offer, but no thanks. I don't do sleepovers." Fine. She'd march out of the room wrapped in a bed sheet if she had to. It wouldn't be the first time, and who knows? Maybe a tabloid reporter would be lurking in the hallway to snap a photo and offer her some much-needed publicity. Dina Joseph still has it. *Take that, Halle Berry. Ha!*

Right.

"Really, I should go," she repeated. Her head swam, dizzy from the lavender and vanilla. A swatch of color caught her eye. *Aha!* She dove for her clothes and scrambled to get them, at the same time wary of Kray and Lane's approach. They remained naked, their cocks still impressive in their limp states, though Dina noticed one straining toward another erection.

She turned away and quickly dressed. *No, don't get horny. These guys are loons.* Great sex or no, it wasn't worth the risk.

"Dina, I don't understand," Kray was saying, "everything was going so well..."

"I knew it," Lane broke in, sounding mournful. "I knew it wouldn't work."

She felt the flush of shock at that remark. Knew *what* wouldn't work? Their plan of seduction, then abduction? Hold her for ransom, even? They'd be lucky to get half the till she made today in payment, as little as Hollywood valued her. And her fans? They'd mourn, then turn their attention to the next phaser-wielding bimbo in go-go boots.

The warning glance Kray shot Lane told her plenty. She had to get out of there before the pain supplanted the lingering pleasure. "Gentlemen," she said, her back straight, "thank you for the lovely evening." Willing her wobbly legs to stiffen, she started for the door.

Kray, however, was too quick, and blocked her exit. Dina's heart pounded, this time out of fear.

"Dina, you have to understand we're not here to hurt you," he pleaded. "If anything, we want to help by giving you the life you deserve."

"I have a wonderful life, and I'd like to continue living it."

Hands cupped her shoulders, and she jumped slightly at the touch. Lane was behind her, trying to soothe her nerves. He was failing.

"Is it...wonderful?" Kray challenged. "You've been stereotyped and reviled by an industry you once worshipped, and you're reduced to these embarrassing appearances at dog-and-pony shows when you could be perfecting your craft --"

"Hey!" Dina snapped. "I'm a damn good actor, thank you very much."

"I never said you weren't. You're a fine actor, and an excellent lover..."

She felt flush at those words, surprised with her reaction to the flattery. Normally she took compliments like these in stride. Other fans fawned, no doubt attracted by her celebrity, whereas Kray seemed to hold more sincerity.

"I knew your potential for both when I saw *The Regal Plot*," Kray continued.

"You saw my film?"

"We both have, many times," Lane said, and she jumped again at his voice. "It's our favorite movie, because you're in it."

No. These men were but children when that film was released, and *The Regal Plot* wasn't suitable for children. It wasn't available on video or DVD, and had never been on television. Dina was amazed enough that Kray knew the title, as she had never bothered mentioning it in her official biography for these conventions.

"H-how?" she asked.

"Dina." Kray came forward and covered Lane's hands with his own. "I have the original film reels, willed to me by the director."

"What? You knew Alan?"

Kray looked at her, the sincerity glowing evident in his eyes. "He was my grandfather, and he loved you very much, as I love you now."

* * * * *

She wasn't buying it. Kray could tell immediately from her reaction. Lane's soft sigh of defeat, wafting in the background, offered little encouragement.

Dina's guarded expression cut deep into Kray's heart. He could almost feel the blood flooding his body, heating his skin at the thought of what was to come. He turned quickly to see Lane appeared equally unnerved, knowing their secrets were to be revealed. For Dina's sake, and for their future, however, Kray knew it was an eventuality they had to face. Premature though it seemed, it had to be done quickly and convincingly.

As many times as he had practiced his words, Kray expected the tremor in his voice. He wanted to cringe. He sounded like a fraud.

"Dina," he said, taking her by the elbow. "Sit." His relief came as small comfort when she did not resist. She perched on the edge of the bed between the two men.

"This is impossible," she was saying. "I knew Alan for years, and he never married or had kids. You can't possibly be his grandchild."

"I'm telling the truth, Dina. Alan Widmark *was* married, for a time, although..." He sighed and pinched his eyes shut for two seconds. How to say this without looking the fool? He would have to be as good an actor as Dina.

"Although," he repeated, "he was not married *here.*"

"Here?" Dina frowned. "Here as in *this hotel*? That makes no sense. You mean, here as in *Toronto*?" She huffed. "You know, if you're married in one place, it sticks wherever you go."

"Dina." Kray shook his head. Her acerbic nature wasn't making this any easier. Best to go for the jugular, he decided. "Dina, pull on my ears. Take them off."

Dina complied, and Kray relaxed and let himself be tugged to and fro in the futile effort. Her cry of fearful surprise hurt nearly as much as her fingers did pinching the pointed outer shell of his right ear.

"We are elves, Dina," he said, "Lane and I. Real, live elves. We are not playing dress up like the others at this convention. This is who we are."

"No," she whispered. "Y-you just used a stronger stage glue for those ears." Her eyes widened, and with trembling fingers, she snatched at one of Lane's ears as if to prove Kray wrong. Lane let out a soft gasp when Dina proved herself incorrect.

"No." *No.* The word sliced Kray's soul in two. How could he convince her?

* * * * *

Okay, now this was *really* getting weird.

Whatever makeup artist they used did quality work. Dina hadn't bothered to notice the ears in detail, but as she tugged stubbornly at them, she noted how seamlessly the outer shells came to a point. The physical anomaly *looked* real, but it couldn't possibly be…

She glanced from Lane to Kray. Their expressions were so sincere, and they wanted her to believe them. Nuts, the both of them. Elves didn't exist. Elves were cartoons that lived in large, hollow trees and baked crackers.

"Why is it so difficult to believe?" Kray asked her. "Your television show dealt many times with issues that seemed impossible for the time. Alien encounters, for one."

"Actors in rubber face," Dina shot back. "That show wasn't filmed on location, you know."

"True, but many theories presented on that show have since come to pass, on the scientific end, anyway," Lane said. His boldness surprised her, as this was truly the first time he asserted himself. "Don't you think it's credible that encounters with nonhuman, sentient beings might come to pass as well?"

"Not in some Toronto hotel!" Dina leaped from the bed and paced its width. "You can't be elves." She pointed at Kray. "And you can't be Alan's grandson. He wasn't an elf! I knew every inch of that man's body. There was nothing pointed on him that wasn't supposed to be pointed."

"Yes, my grandfather was human, and I am half-elven by my mother," Kray supplied. "Alan's son was part of an elven triad."

"So, what, you're saying you're elves from outer space?"

"Not outer space. We were born on Earth," Kray said.

"Really? I'll assume there are more of you on the planet, so how come you don't see more pointed ears these days?"

"You do in our reality," Lane said.

Right. Of course, all the friendly little people in Kray and Lane's reality had pointed ears...and nice white jackets with extra-long sleeves and buckles in the back.

"We are from an alternate universe, Dina," Lane continued, "where our Earth is populated with elves in addition to humans. Our traditions are similar to yours, though because of population concerns many people of both races have taken to mating in threes..." His voice trailed off as he looked down at his naked body, appearing as though he had said too much.

Too much nonsense.

"Dina," Kray said, his head lowered and fingers steepled, "you are familiar with a certain story about a ring, and elves, and other humanlike creatures that sought to destroy the ring?"

"Am I?" Dina snorted. Yet more movies in which she hadn't had a chance in hell of landing a role. "Don't tell me Tolkien was an elf from your bizarro world."

"Not an elf, but yes, he came from our alternate universe," Kray said with casual seriousness. "It certainly explains the realistic quality of the books he wrote. They weren't appreciated as much in our world, and when he and others like him discovered a breach in the space continuum between realities, he took advantage of the opportunity to gain fame through a fresh audience."

Space continuum? This entire conversation read like one of her old scripts. It hadn't make sense twenty years ago, either. "People like him?" Dina frowned. "People like Alan?"

Kray nodded. "My grandfather and his wife sought to find a third with whom they could form their triad. Nobody in his world appealed to him, so he hopped the continuum and met you. Only people who exist in one world and not the other can do that." Kray looked into her eyes and smiled. "There is no Dina Joseph in my world, just as no Kray or Lane or Alan Widmark exists here. Dina, my father told me many times of how you and Alan met. Didn't you think it odd that a man with virtually no credentials or history could get a prominent writing job with a popular television series?"

"It was L.A." Dina shrugged. "If that's the weirdest thing that happened, the town's much better off than I originally thought." To think of it, though, Dina never recalled seeing much of anything personal at Alan's apartment when they dated, on the rare occasions they went there. Alan had been a private man who shared little of his past. Not once, either, had he mentioned a wife in another world with whom he wanted a perpetual three-way.

If Alan had indeed come from another universe, why not share the news with her?

You know why. She shook her head. Yes, she would have dropped him as quickly as her agent had dropped her when her marketability in the business tanked.

"He had hoped to take you back with him, but he was killed before that could happen," Kray said mournfully. "His family barely managed to close his affairs here before anyone became suspicious. When I heard the stories and saw the film" -- Kray raised his chin at this -- "I knew my grandfather would still have wanted you to cross over and enjoy a better life."

Dina snorted. *Right.* She wanted to live in an alternative timeline playing Hollywood has-been to a whole new population of sci-fi fanatics, while spouting tired one-liners on *The Alternate Hollywood Squares.*

"Hear me out, Dina." Kray's voice darkened. "You have no idea how popular your film is in my world."

"What?" She felt the heat of both men closing in on her. Somewhere in the course of conversation, Lane's hand had sought out the sensitive flesh under her arm, and he massaged her. Kray's fingers glided up and down her thigh.

"Everything you hoped for in your career, you can still have; it's not too late," Kray whispered in her ear, then flicked the lobe with his tongue. "You'll star in movies, be adored everywhere you go."

"Best of all," Lane added in her other ear, "you'll have us to love you every night." His breath was warm in her ear. The sensation prickled her skin and stiffened her nipples. There, too, was that familiar ache in her pussy. Dina's senses swam as she grasped hold of the bed's edge and tried to stand.

"No." The concept, of course, was heavenly. To have the successful career, her name above the title, a closet full of awards, had been her dream. To come home every night to two waiting cocks, well, that surpassed any dream script handed her way. She knew, however, no matter how serious these two sounded that it couldn't be true. To drag poor Alan's name into their deceit only hurt more.

She was tired, disappointed, frustrated, and horny. She wanted to believe she had slipped into an episode of *Mission: Jupiter*, but would be happy instead to just crawl back to her hotel room and drink away the memory of having her pussy filled with a pair of divine rods. "I-I'm sorry," she murmured, and dived for the door. "This is just...too much..."

"Dina, no!"

She couldn't tell which one had shouted after her. Stumbling in a heartbroken daze, she kept her eye trained on the door, then the hallway and the bank of elevators. No footsteps followed her; no sharp rapping on her hotel door invaded her sheltered privacy as she slipped into the warmth of her own bed and closed her teary eyes in vain.

* * * * *

"Let her go, Lane." Kray kept his grip across his lover's chest, finding it more impossible to do as the other man fought the restraint.

"We'll lose her."

"We won't. She's not going anywhere," Kray said. "More than likely she'll have extra security at the Q&A panel tomorrow in case we show up, and we will." He felt relieved to see Lane's reserve melt with the simple optimism in his statement. "I know enough about Dina through Grandfather to know that she never backs away from a commitment, no matter how strange the circumstances become."

"She certainly high-tailed it out of here," Lane said with a strained laugh.

"We'll get her back, don't worry. Think of this as another *Mission: Jupiter* episode. The mission is never complete until the last scene. We have time."

Lane eased back on the rumpled bed, his cock resting on his abdomen. He teased Kray with a few gentle strokes to his shaft. "You sound as though you already have a plan."

"I do." Kray knelt between Lane's legs and reached forward to cup the other man's balls. "You know what Mayda Moran always said on that show: 'Never go into battle without a Plan C.' I certainly have that, and because I had the forethought to plan ahead, I now have the time to do this."

He dipped his head forward and took Lane's cock into his mouth, tasting Lane and Dina together, as he knew was meant to be.

Chapter Six

She would take two more questions from these numskulls, then check out of the hotel and get the hell out of here. Never mind that she still had two hours of autographing to do, and that her room was paid for through the next morning, and that Jenna would be miffed, and that her flight didn't leave for another three hours after the hotel's checkout time. Dina was ready to go home *now*.

She hadn't minded before the mild annoyances of answering the same questions about *Mission: Jupiter* con after con after con, but the knowledge that she probably wouldn't be getting any divine fan cock afterward had taken the zest out of today's planned activities.

Should a strapping young man with the qualifications to audition cross her path today, she wouldn't be able to do a thing about it. Kray and Lane had ruined convention sex for her. They had been so wonderful, fucking and sucking her to new heights of ecstasy, but they'd had to spoil everything by turning insane. She knew she had been putting herself at risk in the first place by offering strangers the opportunity to bed her, but last night's experience cemented what she had to grudgingly accept: auditions were officially closed for good.

Head propped on her palm as her elbow slid slightly underneath the weight, she listened halfheartedly to a co-panelist reminisce about a scene he and Dina had flubbed twenty-odd years ago. The crowd chuckled along, clearly understanding more of the story than she did. She couldn't recall the man's face from the sea of extras and bit actors who had passed through the *Mission: Jupiter* set. It stood to reason that his career had met a worse fate than her own.

The panel's moderator called for calm and announced one last question to be directed at her. Dina straightened to attention as hands shot up throughout the small auditorium. She hoped for something simple. She didn't feel like straining to recall details of specific episodes so these guys could settle bets. All she could think about was Kray's cock throbbing in her pussy and Lane's silken shaft sliding past her lips.

All she could think about was how badly she wanted more.

"Okay, I see a hand in the back," the moderator was saying. "You, sir, in the black, come on up to the mic, please."

From the shadows of the auditorium, a tall figure with shocking blond hair emerged. Dina felt her pulse explode as Kray stepped up to the microphone planted several feet before the stage. She wanted to run; she wanted to stay; she wanted the ache in her pussy to subside. She did nothing -- could do nothing -- but watch Kray watch her with an intensity that set her loins on fire.

His words were confident, unlike the other conventioneers who had stumbled over their questions. "Ms. Joseph, I just wanted you to know that I enjoyed your performance in *The Regal Plot*, and I was wondering why you hadn't pursued more films after that."

His knowing smile tested her, taunted her. He knew the answer already. Dina imagined much of the audience did as well, but rather than let herself be shaken by a perceived veiled jab, Dina held her head high and smiled sweetly.

She could still see him naked, his cock like a mast, aching to be inside her.

"Though I enjoyed making *The Regal Plot*, I decided not long afterward that film was not for me. I preferred the more flexible schedule television work offers, so after *Mission: Jupiter* ended, I tried to focus on more roles for the small screen." What a lie that was. "I feel I made the right decision for myself."

"But given the chance, say you were offered the film role of a lifetime...the next Scarlett O'Hara," Kray challenged, "would you reconsider?"

"Uh, sir," the moderator broke in, "you asked your question..."

"I did, and I want an answer." Kray was bold, and held his gaze to Dina's with a strength she swore shortened the distance between them. "Would you reconsider, Ms. Joseph?"

"I would, provided I felt the role was right for me," she said evenly. The rippled murmur of a hundred conventioneers barely fazed her, as did the gruff, nervous *ahem* from her co-panelist. She saw only Kray in the room, clearly offering her a role in his delusion. "Mind you, though, I couldn't take any role in film or television if I felt the story was not genuine."

"How about a love triangle story, with a happy ending for all involved?" Kray had the audience's awed attention. Something about the confidence in his stance and voice kept all eyes on him. Nobody seemed perturbed he was monopolizing the session. Even the moderator returned to his seat, as if bidden there by a spell. "Would you consider a role like that, Ms. Joseph?"

A love triangle...each participant latched to a lover, sucking a cock or licking a pussy. Yes, that she could do again. "It's not implausible; I might consider."

"Okay, say this love triangle is set in an alternate universe, and two members are not considered human. What then?"

This brought the room to life. A hundred different conversations, the participants pondering the logistics of such a plot, rumbled like distant thunder. Dina watched Kray watch her for a reaction and smiled.

"I don't know," she said. "I'd have to read the script, and see the set."

Kray smiled back. "Very well." Without further pretense, he closed his eyes and raised one hand over his head. His mouth twitched in what looked like a silent incantation, and the curious rumblings of the audience spiked with shock when Kray's fingers seemed to grasp the air as one would crumple cloth. Dina gasped when she saw the air above Kray ripple in his fist and tear away.

Shock washed over the auditorium. Cell phone cameras held aloft captured every moment. A lone voice wondered aloud if this was part of the show. Mute from her own shock, Dina couldn't answer.

He was actually doing it. Kray was actually creating a tear in the time continuum. There actually *was* a time continuum, just like the one explained in the *Mission: Jupiter* episode earlier in the session, the one in which she had flubbed lines with her co-panelist...

Dina blinked and put a hand to her mouth. That episode had been written by Alan Widmark.

* * * * *

This, she would have to believe. The look on her face was evidence enough that she was nearly there.

Kray now stood next to a vertical slit from which she could clearly see another place -- a park blanketed in bright green grass in the foreground of an impressive, futuristic skyline. This was Toronto in Kray's world.

He peered through the slit, and a smile split his face as Lane approached from their home world to view Kray's side of the continuum. Lane's appearance caused another wave of excitement among the stunned crowd, Dina included. Kray was happy to see, though, that she was more pleased than upset.

"Here we have your set, Ms. Joseph, and your two costars." Kray gestured to the slit, then to Lane. "Your motivation for every scene would be the knowledge that in this universe, you are admired for your lone film role and that your fans are dying for more work. You have the love of two men who want to see these dreams come true for you. I ask you again, would you reconsider?"

Dina was silent, and stealthy. Kray didn't hear the scraping of her chair against the floor for the pounding in his ears. He couldn't breathe in her scent as she approached for the catch in his throat. Even tired from an obvious lack of sleep, she was still beautiful, more so when she stopped at his side and regarded Lane with a radiant smile.

"It *is* real," she whispered, awed. "Am I dreaming?"

"*I'm* dreaming, Dina," Kray told her. "I've dreamed of this moment of years. I've dreamed the same thing every man in this room has dreamed, and if you cross this threshold with me, everything *you* have dreamed will come true. *We* promise you that." He winked at Lane.

Dina touched his shoulder. Kray felt his cock twitch in response.

"It's beautiful there," she said.

"It is," Lane said. "It's home. It's your reality."

"Home," Dina said.

The word fit perfectly. Kray relished her reaction, and ached all the more. He had to get her across now, and make love with her and Lane. If they made it past the park, he would be showing great restraint.

"I'd consider this role," she said finally, looking at Kray slyly, "if a sequel were guaranteed."

"My lady, that is definitely something we can work out in the contract negotiations." Kray offered her his hand and guided Dina home to a crescendo of whistles and cheers from the audience. Looping an arm through those of her two men, Dina walked farther into the new world as the slit in the continuum quickly sealed shut. Kray noticed she hadn't looked back. Mayda Moran was left behind, but Dina Joseph was here now, and here she would stay and live out her new role.

The background of the crowd's encouragement faded into silence as the veil between the two realities sealed shut. The trio walked to a nearby tree, Kray helped Dina to a cross-legged sitting position against the sturdy, thick trunk.

"Here?" she questioned, looking around the open space. In the park, people dressed similarly to Kray and Lane strolled down gravel paths, while other couples rolled and kissed in the grass, oblivious to prying stares. Kray watched her reaction, and the slow smile brightening her face as she quickly realized that nobody glared or disapproved of the public displays of affection.

"I'm going to like it here," she said.

"I know," Kray agreed.

"So," she said as each man lowered on either side of her, "shall we begin a dress rehearsal now?"

"Dress?" Lane arched an eyebrow. "I was hoping for the opposite."

Dina shot him a playful grin. "I have no problems with that, either." Her body became pliant as Kray and Lane, tugging at buttons and hems, released her from her blouse.

Lane kissed her neck. "Lights."

"Camera." Dina sighed, reaching for Kray's shoulder.

Kray lowered his face to the swell of Dina's breasts, ready to capture an erect nipple.

"Action!"

Excitable

Chapter One

"And then she just...disappeared. There's no other word for it. Disappeared, in the middle of an auditorium full of *Mission: Jupiter* fans." Jenna McCoy wrung her hands tightly, bearing her knotted knuckles against her lap. It looked almost painful, but her attention was focused more on her monologue. Her face exhibited another kind of anguish -- every word spoken revealed her emotions. It looked as though every wince, every wrinkle in her brow, aged her just a little bit. What she had seen, and now relayed, certainly had taken away some zest for life; she seemed that crestfallen.

"It was like something from the show itself," she continued. "One minute, she's on the dais answering the same damn questions she does at every con: what was your favorite episode, who was your favorite guest star, blah blah blah..."

Wild gestures cut the air, and an added eye roll lent the young African American woman a fanatical countenance. All the same, Jeremy thought that, despite her sour expressions, she was rather enchanting. Dare he say it, attractive, even borderline sexy with her pert features, expressive eyes, and short hair dyed bright orange. "Identity crisis" had been the excuse for the drastic change in her appearance, she had said, as her boss's mysterious disappearance two weeks prior had driven her to such extremes.

She babbled on about Dina Joseph's exit from this existence, while his gaze panned first to her smallish breasts, then to the tightened juncture between her thighs made evident in the ripples of her short skirt. Occasionally the hem would creep up the woman's legs and allow Jeremy a view of her shaded, full rump.

Then suddenly his gaze darted upward, and he looked again at her hair. Briefly, the notion of enjoying the view of the rug with the likely mismatched curtains flitted through his mind. *Assuming she didn't shave it off.* Jeremy smiled, then quickly cleared his throat and did his best to maintain a professional air. Jenna was a potential client, not a slab of meat.

"Can you find her?" Her eyes sparkled like dark stained glass. Unshed tears formed a shield that reflected the overhead light of Jeremy's office. The young woman appeared close to ethereal in their somber, wood-paneled surroundings: leather office chairs, bookshelves stuffed with ancient titles he hadn't bothered to read, a framed oil painting of a foxhunt. Aesthetics mostly, for the benefit of clients expecting an atmosphere of professionalism from a private detective. Jeremy cared nothing for it, or for the job; he merely kept up the facade of legitimate work to appease the pack council, all of whom insisted each wolf in the family integrate seamlessly with the general population.

That would change once he was named Alban's successor and he could shed the nine-to-five drudgery that made civilian life so boring. For now, the distraction of the lovely Jenna McCoy made the job tolerable at best.

"You are aware," he began, leather upholstery squealing as he shifted closer to his side of the desk, "that what happened to Ms. Joseph isn't unusual."

"It's not?" Her voice betrayed any attempt to hide her sarcasm. "You'll have to forgive me, then. I was born in Toronto, though I don't live here now, and I'd argue it's not *that* common to see people with pointy ears ripping holes in the fabric of the time continuum."

"Not time, alternate reality. The time continuum is actually a myth, as far as I'm concerned," Jeremy said quite plainly. "Nobody has yet to prove time manipulation is possible, so I'm not inclined to believe it."

She sighed, exasperated, and slouched back in her chair. He could sympathize somewhat; she probably hadn't expected to have such a conversation, and likely hadn't believed in things like elves or alternate dimensions until two such creatures broke with protocol and exposed themselves before a gaggle of sci-fi geeks. Jeremy had heard from Alban that the Federation elders decided in the end to let the matter die. That the indiscretion had happened at a science-fiction convention lent the possibility of the event being part of the show. Meeting with Dina Joseph's assistant, he wondered if Alban or anyone in the Federation was aware that Jenna -- an actual sane person swimming among a sea of Spocks and Sulus -- had witnessed the elves taking Dina.

Or Dina going willingly. Who wouldn't leap at the chance to leave this mundane existence?

"I don't believe it," Jenna said, assertively. "It had to have been some kind of illusion. Smoke and mirrors bullshit. Those men *kidnapped* Dina Joseph."

Jeremy tried not to cluck his tongue to chide her. He should have expected Jenna would grasp for a logical explanation. Most "normals" did when presented with clear evidence of the fantastic. There was always smoke, a mirror, a trapdoor... She probably didn't believe in werewolves, either, never mind that one sat across from her.

Hmmm...

Maybe she could be persuaded to open her mind if he could get her to open her legs to work his own "magic." If he enjoyed anything about his race, it would have to be the ability to manipulate people and things with his active imagination. The hairy, Halloween-mask werewolves of old-time cinema didn't fit the true description of the contemporary werewolf. The *Teen Wolf* movies came close, Jeremy thought, but certainly he had more charisma, and cunning, than what the film portrayed.

Resting his chin on the heel of one hand, he absently waggled the fingers of the other under the guise of stretching. Jenna's reaction was inspiring, and he enjoyed the look of sudden surprise and mild ecstasy on her face. She might be thinking her crossed legs were so tight the pressure affected her clit. She certainly had no idea he had caused the growing tingle in her panties. That excited the werewolf all the more. His cock hardened in his slacks, and he felt grateful for the huge mahogany desk between them. To feel pleasure during a dull workday was always welcome, but such improprieties seldom made for repeat business. Lord only knew how many referrals he'd get from Jenna after she experienced the best orgasm of her life.

"Not necessarily. It's impossible to kidnap the willing," Jeremy said. He traced the alphabet in the air, delighting as she squirmed to every curve and sharp line. He dotted an *I*, and she nearly jumped out of her chair in response to the phantom touch on her clit. "Can I get you something?" he asked, almost teasing. "You look suddenly...uncomfortable."

"I-I'm fine," she stuttered looking about the room. "Hot in here."

The air conditioner ran full blast, and she was in short sleeves. He settled back in his chair and momentarily twined his fingers. She needed a second to rest. "Very well."

"And how do you know Dina went of her own volition?" she demanded. "You weren't there."

That she returned quickly to the subject bothering her didn't go unnoticed. Was he losing his touch, he wondered, if she could switch emotions in the blink of an eye? "But you were there, at the convention. Did you see her struggle or be forcibly removed?" he asked. *Swish.* Jeremy now conducted a symphony with his forefinger. Beethoven's *Eroica*, almost aptly named.

Jenna grasped the arms of her chair and cringed then whimpered. "No..."

"Did she shout for help? She *was* in a crowded hall filled with fans. I'm sure any one of them would have come to her aid if she requested it." He reached an arm forward and drummed his fingers on the desk, rubbing one forefinger in a suggestive manner. She should be feeling the breach to her soaking wet core now, he surmised.

"Uh..."

"Ms. McCoy, it would be unethical of me to take this case," Jeremy said. "For one, you cannot prove Dina Joseph is a victim of kidnapping. Were we able to round up every geek, nerd, and dweeb in the province who attended that convention, they would tell you she went willingly. You said it yourself when you first contacted my office. The police were unwilling to help because they found nobody to corroborate your story. Secondly, I'm not too keen on breaching any alternate dimensions where I don't belong. Besides, with all the different realities out there, it could take years for us to find the one where your Dina now lives. Third, and this is the big one..."

He rested his hand in his lap, brushing his wrist against a thickened erection as his thumb and forefinger rubbed together rapidly. This was going to be a *very* big one; he could tell by the thin trail of sweat gleaming at the young woman's temple. He delighted in her pursed expression and fidgeting manner as she obviously willed her body to suppress the orgasm building inside her.

They were almost home now. This was going to be big with a capital *B*, which rhymes with *C*, and that stands for...

Come...on, man! Dammit!

His fingers stilled with the piercing whistle that filled his ears. Rather than bask in the sound of Jenna McCoy's orgasmic cries, he had to settle for a noise only he could hear, a shrill, private summons from Alban.

His presence was requested at pack headquarters, immediately.

He sighed heavily and released Jenna from his mental hold. The young woman exhaled roughly, and the mocha color returned to her hands as her grip on the chair relaxed. She looked around in a daze, as though waking from a dream. Jenna only seemed to manage a few wheezing syllables before Jeremy willed his erection to stand down so he could rise from his seat. Seeing as it wouldn't go gently into that good afternoon, he grabbed a legal pad and pressed it to his abdomen, hopefully concealing any visible bumps she might spot.

"Ms. McCoy, go home," he gruffly ordered. "I don't doubt Dina Joseph is happier now than she has even been, and if I were to find her, I know she wouldn't want to come back here and spend the rest of her life signing autographs in VFW halls for a dwindling population who can remember when she was an A-lister. Mallory will see you out. I have an appointment I just remembered. No charge for the consult."

You would have charged plenty if I had just five more seconds, he thought with mild annoyance as he bolted out of his office, past his secretary, to the bank of elevators in the hallway. Mallory appeared unfazed by her boss's abrupt departure. Assigned to work for him by the pack, she well understood the eccentricities involved in the job.

Jeremy lumbered through the first set of doors that slid open and turned to face Mallory, who looked up from the game of Internet solitaire she had been playing. She arched an eyebrow and smirked. "*Eroica?*" It was hardly a guess.

He only smiled and let a grand gesture swath the air before him. He took great pleasure in watching his secretary gasp as the elevator closed on her brief ecstasy.

Chapter Two

In accordance with Alban's desire for seamless integration into society, pack headquarters was located on one of the busiest streets in Toronto. On days he was to meet there, Jeremy would normally hop a cable car from his office in the spirit of communing with the "normals," but it would take a while for Alban's ill-timed summons to stop grating on his nerves. He had to wait for sexual satisfaction, so the old man could wait for him. For twenty minutes, Jeremy walked down College Street to Yonge, taking long strides to ease the hard-on bobbing in his slacks.

With his shoulders hunched, he kept his gaze down to avoid eye contact with the multitude of homeless lining the buildings and hiding in the crevices of doorways, blocked from the sun. Occasionally, however, the temptation to peek became too great, and twice on the trek, Jeremy locked on to a Tim Horton's cup filled with change, the owner's elbow propped by a knee. The price of alleviating the sudden twinges of guilt cost him one toony per transient, the last of his two-dollar coins, before he reached his destination.

To the public, pack headquarters resembled a staid edifice sandwiched between an adult video store and a souvenir boutique bearing maple leaf-emblazoned gifts. The interior granted visitors the image of a men's social club that had disbanded on principle rather than succumb to equal-rights admission. Several leather Queen Anne chairs, punctured with gold-plated studs in repeating diamond patterns, bordered an authentic Oriental carpet that spanned the lobby. Wood-paneled walls bore large, gilt-framed portraits of people Jeremy never knew, people he wasn't sure existed in the first place. In fact, nobody in the pack could identify these dour-faced suits with mutton chop beards and walrus mustaches. Rumor had it Alban had bought many of the paintings at various auctions to give people the impression that these men once wandered the building and sipped brandy from large snifters while spinning tales of adventures on safari. Every time Jeremy entered this building, he pictured the room coming to life with these men, not unlike a Disney animated show, complete with a ghost butler bearing cigars on a tray.

The door to Alban's office was on the far end of the room from the front door. He sauntered through the lobby and over the mahogany threshold to find the main players in the pack assembled in an arc around Alban's desk. Richard Leehy, another would-be alpha, offered Jeremy a crooked smile tinted with yellowed smoker's teeth. Next to him stood the ever prim and proper Miss Wallace, the only human employed by the pack to handle various affairs during the full moons. He licked his lips and winked at the older, gaunt woman, hardly surprised to see those thin, pale lips remained set in an unsmiling expression.

To Jeremy's right, he beheld a more welcome vision: the delicious Brenda Braxton, the great hope for the pack's future. A voluptuous creature with more curves than a wayward mountainside road, Brenda looked especially fetching in a soft, low-cut sweater and black pencil skirt. To her immediate right, her mother looked on with restrained disgust.

He smiled. This would well make up for the interruption with Jenna. He had waited long for this day, and the disapproving scowl on Old Lady Braxton's face -- on *all* their faces -- spoke volumes. Alban was going to name his successor. Jeremy would lead the pack and, per his newly gained prominence, and take the sexy, fertile Brenda as his mate to bear perfect cubs for years to come. The notion was certainly enough to get the old lady's goat. He was already looking forward to the first family Thanksgiving.

Alban's snowy white head remained bowed over a sheaf of papers. Jeremy situated himself in the center of the arc, back straight and chin held high as befitting any human keystone, and waited to be addressed. Eager as he was to be rid of the geezer, he was determined to exhibit the respect owed the man. If anything, he realized one day another would think the same of him come retirement, however far into the future that would be.

One last signature nearly sliced a page, and Alban set his work aside. Twining his fingers into a large fist on his desk, the older werewolf peered up at his audience with benign indifference. He regarded Jeremy in particular with a creased brow; there was no love lost between the two. Yet, what choice did the old wolf have? Clearly Jeremy was the only one to lead the pack into a new era. His breeding, his confidence, and his intelligence overpowered everyone in the tightly knit group, likening them all to weakened cubs.

"Jeremy Vanderkellen, this day is a long time coming," Alban began.

Jeremy puffed up his chest. Quickly he recalled the word order of the acceptance speech he had planned since his teens.

The old wolf's voice didn't quiver. "For years, you have been a complete embarrassment to this pack. Your disregard for rules, your disrespect for humans" -- there followed a sideways glance to Miss Wallace, who permitted a slight yet evil smile to bend her lips -- "and your constant public flaunting of paranormal knowledge and abilities continues to put our race at risk."

His posture softened. The ache supported by his smug smile was gone, relaxed as his face fell.

Alban shook his head. "It's a surprise you haven't exposed us altogether with one of your absurd schemes. We should be thankful we're not meeting right now in some cave at the Toronto Zoo while people throw popcorn at us, but rest assured, I'll see to it that never happens."

"What are you saying?" The words sounded hollow coming from his mouth, as though his lips had trouble forming the doubt. His palms began to sweat. No way in hell could Alban pass him over as Head Wolf. This had to be a sick joke.

Yet, the sad nod in his direction only confirmed what Jeremy feared.

"No. You can't do this, Alban." Rage burned in Jeremy's chest. Those around him should thank the gods he wasn't a dragon, he decided. One roar of protest, and this place would have been reduced to cinders in seconds.

The old wolf's voice was cold. "You've given me little choice, Jeremy. You're a loose cannon, and as far as loose cannons go, you make the most inept of us look like Stephen Hawking." He shook his head. Not a strand fell from the shellacked helmet of hair. "I give you this pack, and we're extinct in five years, and I'm being generous with that estimate."

Jeremy thought he heard Miss Wallace mumble, "Six months," but the bitch wasn't worth a rebuttal.

He'd lost the pack!

The prestige, the power, the plans he'd crafted for years while sitting in that damned office pretending to look important flushed down the toilet. Tight fists remained pinned to his sides. No point in using them, Jeremy knew. Flying into a rage would not correct this egregious oversight. "How can you say something like that? Nobody is more qualified to run this pack than I am after you step down."

"I wouldn't say that." If Alban tried to hide the wink offered to Richard, he had done a poor job of it. Maybe it was intentional, but it was enough to set Jeremy's anger several degrees higher. Richard Leehy, Head Wolf!

It took every ounce of control to prevent Jeremy from transforming right there, without the benefit of a full moon. "You. Cannot. Be. *Serious!*" he hissed.

"Like the very heart attack you threaten to give me daily," Alban said coolly. Leaning to one side, he opened a drawer and extracted a manila folder thick with paper that landed flat on the desk blotter with a *thud*.

Jeremy narrowed his eyes. "You have a *file?*" How paranoid was this organization? And hadn't they heard of paperless storage? Alban's office wasn't set for wireless Internet; there wasn't even a computer for a lousy dial-up connection! It frustrated Jeremy how the pack chose to remain in the nineteenth century with regard to procedure...and apparently intelligence, too.

"I have *the* file, son. Every infraction, every stupid scheme, every traffic ticket you've received since you learned to drive, including the one you got squealing out of the Atlanta DMV the day you *got* your license! Never mind what *else* went on in Atlanta, which forced the entire pack to relocate to Canada in the first place. Shall we review some more?" Alban opened the file and held the top sheet between them. "Two years ago, you tried to sue a film company."

"I had a legitimate beef," Jeremy said defensively. "We all did." The film had been a cheesy werewolf horror tale, a gross misrepresentation of their race. As Alban's records indicated, however, the complaint was resolved more to his public embarrassment than benefit.

The next example forced a bitter smile from the older wolf. "Ah, yes. We can't forget last year when you tried to sell werewolf hair clippings online."

"Hey, people go on auction sites and buy haunted cereal boxes. I figured if they're willing to throw away a nickel to buy a quarter, give *me* the money and I'll give them something real."

"I see, and did the money you made benefit the pack?"

Jeremy cast his gaze to the floor. "Actually, I didn't get many bids…"

"No kidding," Alban murmured. "Well, I'd normally enjoy a trip down memory lane, but there's too much here I'd just as soon forget. All the better that this train had never left the station, yet it's a bit late for that. Least I can do is keep it from derailing."

One hard push sent the file crashing to the floor. Nobody around Jeremy flinched, and he had to wonder if this show had been rehearsed, every move of the older wolf expected.

Alban stood and straightened his jacket. "Fact remains, Jeremy, that your constant flaunting of our world puts every wolf at risk, to say nothing of other paranormals." His brows lifted with concern. "You don't know what it's like for me here, son. I have to listen to elves, the fae…there's some vampire who is claiming you've threatened to expose him over an unpaid poker debt!"

"Now, in my defense, that was worth a lot more than what I would have made on the auction site, *and* I would have paid my dues to the pack." Well, some of it, anyway. *Stupid, tightwad, bloodsucking freak.* He had a good mind to visit the sleeping vampire and pull up all the shades.

Alban wasn't listening. "And today you reveal the existence of alternate realities to a normal, setting her under some obscene erotic influence. Are you insane, Jeremy?"

"What? How did you…" But hearing the ever prim, proper, and vindictive Miss Wallace stifle a low-throated murmur answered that. Among her many hats was that of human resources guru. She found jobs for lesser wolves in need of assistance adapting to the human world: retail, hospitality…

…*clerical.*

He pictured Mallory on the phone to headquarters the second the elevator doors closed behind him.

No more orgasms for *her*!

"Wolf magic or not, though I'm certain you had enough sense to cast a memory spell after your shenanigans so the girl would forget everything, the fact remains that you are not fit to lead this pack. Seeing as how Richard is the obvious best alternative, I will hand over the reins to him at the official ceremony at the end of the month." Alban cast a dismissive gesture in Richard's direction, as though the decision were a reluctant one. Jeremy could immediately sense the old man was aware his choice was the lesser man in the room. Why Alban could only see disaster in action he considered bold frustrated Jeremy. With unorthodox measures came risks, and Alban had to understand the pack needed a strong leader to help them survive future generations.

He wanted to shout, swipe the marble knickknacks and blotter from the desk, maybe rip the wispy, black hairs from Miss Wallace's chin, one by one. Instead he kept his cool, his whitened knuckles at his sides. "Alban, this isn't right," Jeremy quietly said.

"No, it isn't." Alban's voice was grim. "You do have a charisma about you, I'll admit to that. But charisma alone doesn't make for a successful leader. Stability is just as important, and Richard has that."

"The charisma of a mollusk," Jeremy muttered. He ignored the glares; he didn't care who heard. It was the truth.

Alban stood and rounded his desk, parting the arc of attendants on his way to the exit. "Well, that mollusk gets to mate with Brenda to assure the perpetuation of the pack."

What? Bodacious Brenda with the pouty red lips mated for life to that melon head? Was Alban trying to breed wolves or dog-show contestants? Jeremy wavered slightly in place, dizzy from the announcement. Around him, people filed silently behind Alban, and he cringed when Richard oh-so-gallantly offered a crooked elbow to Brenda, who gladly took it.

He watched that ruby mouth curl into a smile. Those lips would spend the next several years teasing the soft-serve shaft of that, that...*imbecile!* The mere notion set Jeremy's own cock to stone, just to prove Richard's shortcomings.

"What about me?" he called after the retreating group. "What happens to *me*?"

"Plenty of other eligible ladies in the pack, Jeremy, if any of them would have you," Alban said. "Though I hear you may have burned a few bridges in that department."

Alban moved to leave but lingered at the door, offering Jeremy a piteous glance. "You should take care to prepare for the full moon tomorrow night like the rest of us," he added. "All the extra anger you're carrying, I'd suggest you head for the country now."

"What if I don't want to?" Jeremy challenged. "What if I just wolf out right here in the middle of downtown Toronto on a Friday night? Wreak havoc greater than anything I did in frickin' Atlanta?" He'd do it, too. What was the point in going on if he couldn't lead the pack? Let a Yonge-bound trolley flatten him in the middle of the street for all he cared, but not before ripping through the flesh of a few drunken coeds.

A bemused smile tickled the corner of Alban's mouth. "Oh, I don't think that's going to happen, son. You need to be taught a lesson, something I should have done years ago. You aren't going to harm anybody. You need to learn how to love and respect others, and be truly loved and respected in return."

Jeremy felt suddenly pale. "You're banning me from the pack? How will that help me learn to love and respect others *within* the pack if I can't communicate with them?" Crafty as he was, he knew that without the pack to support him, he wouldn't have long in the world. He'd witnessed official disfellowships while in Atlanta and had heard the news of lone werewolves found slain in the remote woods of northern Georgia by human hunters. With the shunning essentially came an invisible brand on your name. No other werecreature would offer you aid, lest your presence threaten their packs. The pack had educated him, given him work. Sure, he had the smarts to find a job outside the pack, but within brought benefits more valuable to him than any medical or retirement plan.

Was he really that bad of a wolf? Compared to terrorists and serial killers? He sued a movie studio; he didn't try to blow it up. "You can't do that."

The older man shook his head. "I'm not that cruel. However, if you want confirmation that you're in the doghouse with everyone here, you'll get it soon enough." And Alban slid slowly out of view.

"Doghou --" Jeremy huffed. "What is *that* supposed to mean?"

The old wolf poked his head back into the room and grinned. "It means you're not the only one here who's crafty with his magic."

Chapter Three

Normally, Jenna disliked crowded, cacophonous bars, and consequently nixed any offers to club hop with friends and dates. Tonight, as she lounged in a molded wire chair on the open-air back patio of The Orbit Room, she was grateful for the blast of jazz-rock fusion sweeping through the narrow hallway that led to the main bar. The music served a good purpose in drowning out the irritating blind date set up for her.

Six sheets to the wind and halfway to the seventh, the heavy-lidded man with the French-Canadian accent offered her a crooked smile before planting an oft-toked joint between his lips. Where he'd gotten it, she couldn't be certain; it was past one in the morning, and the place was packed. Any of a hundred mouths, cold sores and all, could have touched that thing. She refused her turn, opting for a somewhat safer contact high as Malcolm blew the smoke in her direction.

Malcolm? Or was it Mario? Or Martin?

Jenna didn't catch his name when her next-door neighbor introduced them, only grabbed her purse when he showed up and let him drag her all over the city. She had hoped the evening would help lighten her mood, help her to forget the disappearance of her former boss and friend. Help dispel any notion that she might be losing her mind.

She took a long pull from her dewy bottle of Sleeman's and leaned back to watch the cirrus clouds thread farther across the sky and envelop the full moon in a wispy gauze. The night had proven useless, more so than the past few days. Authorities in Toronto had been unable to help her any further with the case. Scratch that, there *was* no case according to them. Nobody seemed to remember Dina Joseph disappearing into thin air, escorted by two *Mission: Jupiter* fans...nobody except her. All pictures taken at the event, digital or otherwise, had somehow managed not to develop. She had no proof of Dina's abduction other than her memory, which nobody seemed to trust.

She wasn't entirely sure now *she* could trust it. But, Dina wouldn't have just abandoned her in a convention hotel. Jenna had been invaluable to her, securing Dina numerous personal appearances at fan conventions around the world. Sure, the gigs weren't as glamorous as A-list movie roles, but they made good money. Dina was just happy not to be relegated to dinner theater costarring alongside other television has-beens. And Jenna had loved working for her; she thought the feelings had been mutual. More than once, Dina had even expressed explicit, intimate feelings.

So how could an entire auditorium full of people not remember the air splitting in two to reveal another world? Jenna badly needed to know the answer, so much so that she called her roommate in Santa Monica to let her know she planned to stay indefinitely in Canada until she could find closure. Luckily, a cousin leaving for an extended vacation abroad allowed her use of his place rent free. Two weeks later, nothing. Nobody at the con proved helpful, the police would do nothing without more solid proof, and that detective... *Ugh*.

She closed her eyes and inhaled. The cannabis smoke was sweet and pungent, and she relished the dizzying sensation that veiled her mood and tingled her skin. Normally, a good fuck would provide an excellent complement to the high, but Malcolm-Mario-Martin didn't appear to be a sponge-worthy candidate.

Then again, this was only her second beer -- she didn't have the constitution for these potent Canadian brews -- and one in the morning was relatively early on a Toronto weekend.

Malcolm-Mario-Martin leaned into her, smelling of Bob Marley's aftershave. "How 'bout some pizza?" he buzzed into her ear so she could hear over the din. "We'll try that place across the street."

"Do I have to move?" Her body was leaden. "Can't we get chicken wings or something?"

"They closed the kitchen. C'mon."

Grabbing a full Sleeman's Cream Ale from the tray of a passing waitress, Jenna followed her date through the narrowing passageway leading to The Orbit Room's main bar. Down the stairs, across the street, and weaving around scattered tables, she found a space by the window of the corner pizzeria and downed the beer while Malcolm-Mario-Martin ordered slices. From her front-row seat, she watched Toronto nightlife in full bloom -- everybody laughing and chattering and toasting life, blissfully unaware that one of them might no longer have the luxury to do the same.

She felt a chill not associated with the drink or smoke. She closed her eyes to expel the thoughts from her head. Jenna didn't want to accept the possibility that Dina Joseph might be dead. Bizarre as the departure had appeared, Dina had looked happy. Those weirdos who had taken her seemed enamored by her. If only she could remember what that detective -- the third one in the city she had contacted -- had told her...

Ugh. Her stomach roiled at the memory of that smarmy private eye. The memory of their meeting was blurred, but Jenna knew she would never forget his condescending manner and leering appraisal of her. More than that, there had been an aura about the smirking, yet uncannily handsome, man. He'd offered her no help in finding Dina, and Jenna had the impression he seemed to know more than he let on.

If only she could *remember.*

Just thinking back to yesterday's appointment caused her head to hurt and, for some reason, her body to tingle with want.

Blech. Please tell me I'm not attracted to that man. A night with any of Dina's Klingon-chanting virgins would be preferable.

The pizza helped little in easing any physical and mental discomfort. What little she did eat tasted like cardboard and canned sauce. Her date, now etched in her mind as 3-M, downed his plate and most of hers in five bites.

He licked specks of cornmeal from his fingers. "Y'wanna 'nother beer?"

His handsome, stubbly face stretched and yawned in her intoxicated vision. If she tilted one way, the man resembled a darker version of Jeremy Vanderkellen, Private Detective, somewhat, and Jenna cringed inwardly to feel her nipples tighten in response to this observation. Lolling her head to other side distorted the view, but not the memory of Jeremy's curled, endearingly creepy smile as she recalled his piercing gaze scanning her legs.

Guh. She would have to fuck 3-M just to cleanse the palate.

"Glass of wine, then?" he suggested. "A Coke?"

"Sure." She smiled, drooping her lids to tighten her vision of 3-M, as though concentrating to will X-ray vision. She wanted to see her date's chest. An odd indentation at nipple height indicated a piercing of some sort. Suddenly, she wanted to run her tongue up and down the silver stud hidden by the tiny horse patch stitched to the breast of his shirt. She wanted to live now that Dina Joseph could not be here to do so.

She wanted to fuck and forget, if only for one night.

"So, what'll it be?" 3-M pressed. "A Coke?"

Jenna shook her head. "A cock," she said. Damned if she were overheard. She *wanted* to be overheard. She wanted people to know she was alive, and now would be living double-time to make up for what Dina missed. If that meant fucking a guy she'd just met to ease ill thoughts of some worm, so be it. "A cock and a smile."

3-M proudly delivered the latter, tossed a toony on the table for the busboy's tip, and pulled her out of the pizza joint so they could catch a passing trolley.

* * * * *

Jeremy sat naked in his favorite leather lounger, turned to face the broad picture window overlooking the city. From his living room on the twentieth floor of his building, he could nightly soak in the flickering landscape of Toronto. Weekends, especially, seemed brighter, with views of the Canadian National Tower and the ballpark's lights marking activity. He slouched down a few inches, smiling as the sensation of leather against flesh cooled him.

In ten minutes the moon would rise, and he would change. Then Toronto would face its most devastating terror since the SARS outbreak. Tonight, a wolf would prey among the innocent and weak, stalking partygoers and unsuspecting drunkards stumbling from pub to pub. As the rest of the pack frolicked and howled in some national park, a lone wolf would cripple the city...because he knew he could.

If he were to be captured or killed, no matter. What was his life without the assurance of assuming pack leadership? He had no mate, no prospects of finding one, he hated his job, and he didn't much care for others in his pack. If there was anything positive to come out of being passed over for Head Wolf, it was that he wouldn't have to deal with Miss Wallace. Then again, he *could* make life miserable for her, or invite her on a campout during the next full moon...

He scratched the arms of the chair. The tingling sensation that signaled the change twinkled in the pit of his stomach, slowly spreading erotic warmth through his veins. Jeremy's cock hardened, quicker than before, given the situation, at the prospect of changing. Breaking the rules had always stimulated him to some extent, but never before had he felt so aroused, so alive.

A wolf in the city, with nobody to stop him. No nattering Alban, no whining Richard. He salivated and twisted in his seat, already tasting the blood and flesh he'd devour by night's end. He flicked an aching incisor with the tip of his tongue, nearly cutting the sensitive flesh when his doorbell sounded.

In all the time Jeremy had lived in Toronto, he couldn't recall *anybody* using the doorbell, much less knocking. He never sent out for food; any wolf-related summons came via the call that pierced his eardrums. For everything else, people contacted the office.

Who would be calling him now, just minutes before the full moon?

Alban? Alban might anticipate that Jeremy would do something rash, but the old wolf towed the line too well to remain where people could be at risk. He wouldn't do anything so foolish as to leave another wolf behind to see to Jeremy, either.

"All right, already," he growled at the second chime. A cold sweat broke across his forehead. He limbs felt heavy as he neared the door. His toes curled and the bones creaked, ready to stretch into paws. God save the poor, inept pizza boy on the other side of the door, ringing the wrong address. In a matter of minutes, Jeremy would have one pie with *everything*.

Instead, he was surprised to encounter the thin-lipped Miss Wallace staring dourly back at him. Not a hair out of place in her graying bun, the spinster held her awkward stance, as if somebody had shoved a pole up her ass and let her dangle.

Jeremy bared lengthening fangs in order to mask being taken aback. "Death wish, Miss Wallace?"

She huffed and stepped past him into the living room. "I've come for satisfaction, Vanderkellen, and I don't intend to be disappointed."

"Well, I'm certainly dressed for the occasion." He gestured to his upright hard-on. Tufts of hair, which he normally kept shorn, sprouted around the base. "I have to say, your timing kind of sucks. In a few minutes, I'll be a full-fledged wolf with an appetite for destruction, and you'll be the first course."

Miss Wallace perched her small bottom on the arm of the leather chair and patted her purse. "Oh, I have a snack for you right here, Vanderkellen. And I'm not afraid of you."

"Really? What did you bring, a silver bullet?"

"Guns are barbaric," Miss Wallace retorted. "I have other means of protection when I'm out alone."

"Yes, that face alone must work wonders at scaring would-be muggers. You know, you're a fucking *loon* to come willingly to a wolf's lair on the night of a full moon."

"Alban has assured me of my safety."

"You'd be safer with Alban here wolfing out instead of me. That neutered old fool. Of course, you'd know that already since you fuck him."

"Fuck *you*," Miss Wallace snapped.

"Maybe. If I don't kill you first." The words were delivered with more spittle than usual. It was becoming hard to talk, even more difficult to comprehend what Miss Wallace was saying. The wolf in him grew strong, demanding release. Beyond the view of Toronto, he spied the glowing ball of light emerging from a string of gauzy clouds. No time to warn Miss Wallace; he was going to change.

And Miss Wallace crossed her legs, sheathed in support hose, and checked her nails. The witch.

It was his last conscious thought before the transformation, those precious seconds when passion derailed logic. The initial twinge of change now possessed every nerve in his body, strumming a tune that tweaked his nipples and tugged his cock, and set his senses on fire. He arched backward and relaxed, letting the moon work its magic on his body. The end result often yielded a more orgasmic beginning to the evening. The pleasured pain of claws extending from his fingers, the reshaping of his torso into leaner, canine muscle, and the enhancement of his sight and olfactory perceptions brought welcomed release. In wolf form, he became faster, stronger, sleeker.

He liked it.

He crumpled to the floor and outstretched every limb. His skin exploded with hair, his nails lengthened and thickened, and a guttural cry bubbled in his throat and released with a mighty…

Yip! Yip yipyipyipyipyipyip!

Something was wrong.

Lean, terrible paws should have crossed his line of vision. He should have been ready to flip over and pounce on Miss Wallace to show her truly that Alban had been wrong to let her come here. Instead, he was aware of being smaller than usual. Lighter, too. Whatever the result of this transformation, it was over and he could think straight again.

He took a few steps, conscious of the *tap tap tap* of little toenails against hardwood. What had happened to his stealth pace?

He looked down and found the answer in two tiny paws.

Shit!

He went skittering down the hall to his bedroom. The full-length mirror tacked to the closet door confirmed the worst. Alban hadn't been joking the day before about magic, and punishment. Never, though, had he thought the old wolf would do something so humiliating.

He was a *Chihuahua*. He was a fucking *lapdog*!

From behind came the heavy footfalls of sensible shoes. Miss Wallace towered over him like the spinsterly older sister of a fairy-tale ogre. Jeremy caught a brief glance of granny panties while looking up her skirt and tried to gag.

"Oh, is widdle puppy not well?" Miss Wallace cooed, laying it on thick. From her purse, she produced a doggie treat. "Does widdle puppy want a Milk-Bone?"

Jeremy answered by lifting his leg over her shoe.

Chapter Four

Fingers everywhere. Exploring threads, searching for zippers, poking ribs. One struck nerve sent a shockwave of pain down Jenna's leg, and she reacted with a swift heel to 3-M's shin as he stood behind her.

"Watch it!" he warned, squealing. "If you hit certain parts, they might not work."

"Well, we can't have that," she murmured, now regretting her earlier bravado. The Sleeman's had worn off during the glacially slow trolley ride to her apartment building, and as they stood on the stoop while she fumbled with her purse, she felt all previous horny feelings slide slowly to her feet. The mood was fading with the soft passage of clouds trying to conceal the full moon. How she would get rid of 3-M, she didn't know. She didn't have a roommate, so there went that excuse.

Of course, 3-M was so keyed up now. Jenna could feel his erection brushing her backside as she dug into her purse. He would have likely turned the inconvenience of a third party into an opportunity, anyway. She sighed and wondered what would happen if she just lay there while he humped her. Would he even notice her lack of interest?

3-M wrapped his arms around her waist and nibbled her neck. His tongue tangled in her short hair and hoop earring, and he tugged it until she jerked her head away. The thin metal post in her lobe held fast, and she winced from the pain her unfortunate move caused.

"Uh, ow?" came a retort dripping with sarcasm that 3-M clearly couldn't sense for the influence his raging hormones now had over him. He crushed her to him, rocking her in a disruptive rhythm that jarred her eyesight and created an involuntary palsy preventing her from extracting her keys from her purse. She felt like a human claw in a machine at a kiddie pizza parlor, so close to snatching the prize but failing to get it two inches past the pile of stuffed animals and fake Rolex watches.

Some prize. Why the urgency over getting into her apartment, she wondered. True, she wanted to go home, only alone now. She'd get off, but if anything would aid her in reaching that goal, it would be a toy from the bag she kept in the closet, not this steaming, drunk irritant behind her.

"You anywhere close yet?" he whined in her ear. Jenna was thankfully his lips only brushed the outer shell this time rather than tried to devour it.

"Close to the edge," Jenna grumbled. She was teetering on the cusp of insanity with this clown prodding her to swan dive. Her head throbbed, her body crumpled forward inch by inch, trying to rebuff 3-M's advances. *How does one retract an invitation for sex without appearing too rude?* She contemplated a solution when a sharp yipping noise broke her thoughts.

"What's that?" She managed to wrench herself from his grasp and move away from the door. The sight of a trembling Chihuahua at the foot of the brownstone steps tore at her, and her heart softened.

"Oh, hello, boy," she cooed. 3-M was completely forgotten. "It's past your bedtime. Are you lost, fella? Huh?" Her mood turned suddenly giddy as the tiny dog wavered on quivering legs and looked up at her with soulful, dark eyes. Poor thing, lost in the middle of Toronto... She saw no collar to give hint of any identification. The Chihuahua appeared to be purebred, hardly a stray mutt, so how did it become lost?

Squatting down to its level, Jenna held out her arms and warmed as the dog quickly skittered into her embrace. At least something might go right this week. She might not be able to help Dina, but maybe she could give this dog a home for a few days until its owner could be traced.

"Hello?" 3-M sang, bumping her from behind. "We gonna fuck or what?"

"Why don't you start without me?" she snapped and tried to muscle past him to the door. With the dog looped under one arm, she used it to block 3-M as she retrieved her keys. The Chihuahua, sensing her dislike for her date, bared its tiny fangs at the sleepy-eyed dolt.

"Ehhh, watch it." 3-M sneered at the dog and stepped closer until he was literally breathing down her neck. "What's with the one-eighty? I thought you wanted to have some fun."

"That was the Sleeman's talking. I tend to stay mute on a first blind date. Sorry to have disappointed you." *Please, let him be gracious enough to accept that,* she prayed, *or at least miss my face when he spits.*

"No, beer can't talk. *You*, on the other hand, said quite a bit..." The scowl curled upward, and a malicious laugh pounded in her ears. Her heart froze. She clutched the dog close for protection. Surely he wouldn't consider taking her by force? Drinking or not, he was her neighbor's friend, and though Jenna had met the woman across the hall only a few times, she figured she wasn't one to socialize with lecherous types.

"I said watch it!" She pinned the dog to her chest, but it appeared the Chihuahua had other plans. The tiny dog squirmed in her grip, bracing its paws against her arm to push upward. Hind legs kicked and scraped at her until she finally relaxed her grip. The dog landed on its feet and scurried around the couple.

3-M chortled. "Looks like you've been dumped, babe."

He wasn't laughing, however, when the tiny dog sprang upward and bit him on the ass. Jenna lurched backward as her date yelped and twisted from side to side, swatting aimlessly. The dog had a vise lock on 3-M's lower left buttock and growled as its fangs sank deeply into the denim. She had to laugh at the sight.

"It's not funny, bitch!" 3-M cried, swiping air as the dog managed to swerve out of reach. It seemed nothing could dislodge the miniature terror...except a hasty, heartless apology, delivered on a labored sigh.

At that, the dog's jaws widened, and the Chihuahua landed gracefully at their feet.

"Good night, Malcolm, or Mario or Martin or *whatever* the hell your name is." Having found her keys, Jenna unlocked the door and ushered the dog inside. "I got a better deal."

She was halfway up the stairs, Chihuahua in tow, when she thought she heard the man scream, "My name is Manuel!" Like it mattered to her. She hadn't planned to add him to her Christmas card list.

Chapter Five

The last half hour, his first thirty minutes in this new state, had been a blur. Urinating on Miss Wallace's foot had earned him punishment in the form of being kicked out of his apartment and into the next waiting elevator heading south. Just his luck, none of his nosy neighbors had bothered to check on the commotion outside, clearly uninterested in the blatant disrespect toward animal rights.

Ignoring the look of surprise on the doorman's face, he skittered out of the building and into Toronto. Jeremy was only concerned with finding safety from that dog-hating witch. The second he changed back into human form, he would make note to inform Alban of his lover's decided loathing of the canine species. See if the old wolf would fuck her doggie-style then!

From this ant-high view, the city looked completely different. Buildings stretched like reeds into the night sky. Lumbering, thick feet plodded along sidewalks, barely noticing his tiny body in their path. He must have yipped himself hoarse alerting pedestrians of his presence, and merely growled at anybody who reached down for a conciliatory pat.

"Whatsa matter?" drooled one drunken blonde, her tanned breasts about to spill from her low-necked blouse as she bent down to his level. "Do you want a Scooby snack?" Gay tittering from friends filled the air around them.

He wanted a snack, all right, and licked his sandpaper tongue across his jowls. Those ample melons beat any sack of kibble. He jumped in hope of nipping a ripened tip between his teeth, but the woman, sotted as she was, was still too quick. The group laughed into the throng of night revelers, leaving the were-Chihuahua to fend for himself.

Keeping his head down, nose to the sidewalks, he got lost easily in the different neighborhoods. Faint landmarks illuminated by streetlamps offered clues to his whereabouts. Rainbow flags flapping in the breeze denoted passage through the gay district at Church and Wellesley, which irritated him. As a human, he wouldn't have been caught dead here. Random turns took him past St. Michael's, the seat of the archdiocese, and eventually to Yonge. For a little dog, he'd certainly gone a long way.

And his feet were killing him.

When he could take it no longer, he came to a rest against the steps of a brownstone. The name of the street mattered none to him; he just wanted to curl into a tan crescent and sleep off this nightmare. If he awoke naked on a deserted Toronto street, all the better. He'd be picked up by the police, and he'd reveal every paranormal secret from the werewolves to the fae to all the undead, flesh-eating, stealth-winged creatures that lived among normal folk. Sure, he'd be locked away as a loon, but he'd have privacy. Screw the pack, maybe he didn't need them after all, if they were going to treat him like this.

He whimpered into the concrete and spat away dust and pebbles. Why didn't they like him? *Why doesn't anybody like me?* He remembered Brenda didn't appear too disappointed to learn she wouldn't have to mate with him, and Miss Wallace...well, maybe she didn't like any of them!

He, unfortunately, had to find somebody to love. Alban had said so, and for all his derogatory remarks about the old man, Jeremy couldn't really deny Alban's wisdom. Being transformed into a lowly fast-food mascot was more than just a one-night punishment. Maybe this was a curse that could only be broken at Alban's discretion. If so, Jeremy had sorely misjudged the old wolf's power. Truly, it had strengthened with age and wisdom.

Watching the activity at the front door above him, Jeremy found new vigor in his increasing anger. Some asshole was badgering a lady, not cool. Even at his most cad-like, Jeremy liked to think he knew when to back off. This guy obviously couldn't spell the word *no*, much less comprehend its meaning.

Yip! Yipyipyipyipyip! Damn this falsetto alarm! He wanted to cringe, but the barking was enough to attract the woman's attention. Jeremy felt his tiny canine heart palpitate when he saw who his distressed damsel was.

Jenna McCoy, the potential client from earlier. He had played an invisible symphony on her clit, and wished to do much more. Perfect timing, stuck in this form. He had to suffice with being crushed against her warm chest as she made sickening baby noises.

Get it out your system, he bade her silently, panting.

Her unwanted companion, threatened by the pint-size usurper, made a move that Jeremy quickly quelled by animal instinct. One chomp on the ass dispelled any thoughts of the jerk's continued harassment. The next thing he knew, he was happily, albeit uncomfortably in this unfamiliar form, struggling up the stairs to Jenna's apartment.

"C'mon, boy," she cajoled, and Jeremy hoped she would bend down to pick him up. If she thought her high-pitched encouragement was any better than a lift...he shook his little head and tried to push all thoughts of frustration away. He'd lost track of time, but the heavy mist outside indicated the possibility of the coming sun. Maybe in thirty minutes or so he'd transform back into his naked, human form and show her that she had indeed brought the correct suitor home.

"In you go." She ushered him into a cramped loft, its walls lined high with overstuffed bookshelves. Billowy sofas, bordering a large Oriental carpet, faced each other in the main living area. Oddly shaped sculptures dotted the apartment's landscape. He surmised Jenna had picked the pieces at random to give visitors the impression that she had some fascination for art. A well-placed broomstick would have looked equally fashionable in the otherwise dull room.

He leaped onto one sofa, nearly sinking into oblivion as the thick, downy cushions threatened to swallow him. He yelped, but was unheard for the banging of distant cupboards.

"I don't have much for doggies to eat," Jenna called from the kitchen, "but I can give you a dish of water. Oh, and I have some beef jerky somewhere. Maybe you can eat that?"

The cushion muffled the gargling sound in Jeremy's throat. Yummy. *Can I hope for a linen napkin to dress this feast?*

She set a cereal bowl filled to the brim at the edge of the carpet. Not to seem rude, Jeremy hopped off the couch for a few obligatory licks. To be truthful, the long trek had parched him, but he didn't dare touch the dried meat left next to the bowl.

Jenna had taken the other couch and was removing her shoes. She tucked her feet underneath her rump and sighed. "Don't worry if you mess anything up. It's not my furniture. I tell you, dogs have it so good."

Don't count on it. At least as a human, he could pick up utensils and wipe his own ass.

"You don't have to pay rent, or taxes, or work for a living." She sighed again and leaned back. Jeremy could see her bustline as her chest heaved up and down. She stretched completely on the sofa now and idly picked at her blouse. Suddenly his cereal bowl oasis didn't look as enticing.

"You sleep in the sun, you shit on the floor, and it's not your problem. Somebody always comes by to clean it up." Her voice took on a darker tone. "You probably don't miss people who leave you, either. Always somebody else to come along with treats." She rolled onto her stomach and smiled painfully at him. "You'll forget me, too, I'll bet, once we find out where you belong."

Not true. Jenna was lovely to behold, so vulnerable and melancholy. He suddenly felt bad for having toyed with her during their meeting. She could only be referring indirectly to her friend, the actress. A quick scan of the room revealed a few framed photographs of them. Though a mere Chihuahua, he thankfully had retained his primed wolf vision, and could easily tell many of shots highlighted Dina and Jenna's camaraderie.

"I'm not going to let myself get too attached to you," Jenna warned, "because you're so damn cute. I've already lost one best friend. I can't bear to have anything else I love taken away."

Any sympathy he tried to convey came out in a foreign whine. She giggled as she slid off the couch and scratched the scruff of his neck. The touch was pure heaven. "You sleep anywhere you like, hon. The couch is really comfy. We'll get you home in the morning." With that, she padded down a short hallway to a backroom and left the door open just a hair.

Jeremy didn't move for the couch, but slithered to the floor and rested his chin on his paws. Amazing how looking at someone through different eyes elicited different feelings. As a werewolf, he naturally didn't come into contact with people, but acted out his primal needs in remote woods. Here, as a simple dog, he seemed to see more than that jerk did outside earlier.

Jenna was a woman in pain, and he wanted nothing more right now than to take it away.

The air was silent for a minute. He fixed his gaze on the sliver of light spilling from her room. An occasional shadow indicated movement, presumably as she prepared for bed. The urge to tiptoe closer for a peek of cocoa flesh was strong, but in this new state of sensitivity Jeremy felt conflicted. Quite obviously, he realized, Alban cursed him so to show him that he had been a cad. Spying on Jenna would certainly confirm that. Maybe, in staying put, he would earn the love he needed to break the curse.

His ears perked up at the sound of a faint buzzing, followed by a low, pleased moan.

Dear God. Jenna was using a vibrator.

He was at the door in two seconds.

Chapter Six

The second the cool, hard plastic tip touched skin her pussy twitched. Yet Jenna ground her upper teeth into her bottom lip and tried to focus on more pleasant pursuits. That she had let loose a prospective lover -- irritating, he was, but a man was a man -- in favor of this battery-operated substitute niggled at her. If only the alcohol hadn't worn off, she might be warmer in this bed, and wriggling underneath a hard, seductive body as a thick cock pounded into her and helped her forget her troubles.

Of course, she'd wake up with a monstrous headache and many regrets. She tried to convince herself she had done the right thing while repeating in her mind that 3-M's cock probably wasn't as big as the buzzing lavender tool now teasing her clit.

Mmmm. Braced against the headboard, knees raised and spread wide, Jenna played with one hardened nipple while her other hand directed the vibrator so she could reach orgasm. Up and down, the hard shaft massaged her nether lips and dipped slightly into her aching core, greased by her own juices. Normally, when in such a state, she was content to just press the vibrating plastic to her clit and ride an orgasmic wave to shore. Tonight, however, a quick fix wouldn't do. It would take a long time to get over the realization that her life wouldn't be the same. One little spurt couldn't soothe that pain.

Dina wasn't coming back.

Nobody was going to help Jenna find her.

She would have to get another job.

And now she had to take care of somebody's dog. She sighed. Well, that last part wasn't exactly a burden. Perhaps, in some divine way, the Chihuahua's appearance was a blessing. She had taken care of Dina for so many years, seeing to appointments and conventions; maybe she could transfer that support to a creature of greater dependence.

The thought perked her up a bit. If nobody claimed the dog, she decided, she would take it in and give it a real home, and a name.

First, however, she had to take care of herself.

She plunged the vibrator deep inside her, twisting slightly to reach her spot. Failing, she opted for the quick fix and pressed the shaft to her parted lips; the tapered tip flicked rapidly against her clit. Wonderful as it felt, the orgasm was slow in arriving. Jenna's mind was a jumble of woes and concerns, and a brief temptation to give up passed as she decided she was too distracted.

Come on, she urged the toy, and closed her eyes. There had to be something, some erotic image or fantasy, she could use to dispel the dark clouds haloing her aura.

She thought of Dina, beautiful and ageless beyond her renown from a decades-old television series. The two had dabbled in minor activities during wild convention parties, yet neither woman considered herself gay, or bisexual. For Jenna, anyway, there was no attraction to women in general, just to Dina's peerless beauty and vivid personality. It was no wonder the cult actress was able to lure second-generation fans so easily to her bed.

And two had lured her away for good.

She conjured a wavering specter of Dina in her mind, willing the image to kneel before her parted thighs for a taste of ripened, wet fruit. Using the vibrator to simulate the action, Jenna guided the quivering tip up and down her swollen lips and traced an oval pattern before dipping low to tease her backside. She imagined Dina's tongue following the same route, tapping at her clit and easing hooked fingers into her slit in search of that elusive spot. The contrived memory helped as blossoming ecstasy boiled in her belly and warmed her blood. An orgasm would be quick to wash over her.

Quite suddenly, the lovely visage of Dina hardened into a decidedly masculine form. Her eyes still clamped shut, she continued her ministrations as Dina morphed into Jeremy Vanderkellen.

Huh?

It shouldn't have come as a complete surprise. She had thought of the man off and on over the past several hours. Despite his brusque manner, he *was* handsome, and probably had a libido to match his swaggering personality. No doubt the detective would have given 3-M a run for the money in the bedroom.

Nestled between her legs, a naked Jeremy stretched forward and grasped either side with his ghostly fingers. Jenna watched his bare bottom jounce on the mattress when he dived for a long, exploring taste.

"Nice, Jeremy," Jenna murmured aloud. "How about we play some more?"

*****

That, I can definitely do…
…when the sun comes up.

Jeremy kept his nose lodged between the door and the jamb, picking up the sharp scent of Jenna's arousal. Even in the dim, his keen eyesight easily detected her solo play, and he watched with frustrated delight as she rocked and stroked herself to a frenzy. That he couldn't join her and make the evening more pleasurable was pure torture; then again, he supposed he should be thankful to Alban for allowing this to happen. Otherwise, in his regular wolf form, he would likely be dodging patrol cars and tranquilizer darts.

The only advantage to his current state was that Jenna couldn't see him spying on her. If she did, it clearly didn't bother her much. A human Peeping Tom, probably not so welcome, even though she'd called him by name.

Jeremy perked up; his ears straightened. That's right! She'd called for him. She was thinking about him while beating off.

Nice.

Of course, it wasn't the love Alban had intimated before the curse was cast, so who knew how this would affect future transformations. For now, though, being a Chihuahua wasn't half-bad. For the night, he had a warm place to stay and a free show. Adding love to the equation would have been a bonus. Now that he knew Jenna had some interest in him beyond his alleged professional talents, he decided to get in touch with her before the next full moon.

She giggled, as though drunk, and continued to caress herself. Her hand glided under the swell of one breast and lifted it so she could lick her own nipple. Jeremy felt his entire body stiffen at that. Oh, if only this were ordinary time.

"Jeremy..." She sighed. The dog's high-pitched whine followed. Not just out of want.

He twitched. He hurt, seriously. His limbs, his teeth, and even his nose, twinged with a pain akin to have tumbled down a flight of stairs, coupled with few sledgehammer blows. This was not an uncommon sensation, either, but one Jeremy experienced...

...when changing back. Being so small, the pain was amplified to reflect the rapid growth of a foot-long Chihuahua into a grown man.

Shit! How could this happen now? Not once in his memory could he recall having the ability to change under a full moon. Such powers did exist, however, as special traits of those destined to rule as Head Wolf.

So...did he have this skill, or did another power assist in this transformation? Was Alban involved?

He tried to clamp his jaws shut so as not to alarm Jenna, but eventually the need to release the strain of changing surpassed any outside concerns, and he morphed back to human form, complete with a loud roar. Unlike his normal shift from human to wolf form, he was conscious of all changes here. Pain seared his body in one brief, powerful explosion then quickly subsided when all traces of the lapdog disappeared. Feeling boneless, he curled to the floor and hoped for the strength to stand.

On the other side of the door, he heard appliances crash to the ground as the young woman squealed. Heavy footfalls signaled to him that she was probably covering herself, or looking for a weapon.

"Who's there?" she screamed. "Manuel? I'm calling the police."

"No, don't. Please." Testing his human legs, Jeremy rose slowly but stumbled. Naked and apprehensive, he wanted to remain hidden from Jenna's sight. "Don't get up. I have the wrong apartment. I'll leave."

"Wrong what?"

He backed away a few steps and touched the front doorknob, but remembered he wore nothing. He tried to recall if Jenna had an afghan draped over one of her sofas, but the woman had thrown open her door and flicked on the hallway light. The sudden explosion of white burned his eyes, and he shielded them from view.

"What the --" He lowered his arm, and in seconds his eyes adjusted. He saw Jenna's gaping expression. She was still naked, but clutched a spike-heeled shoe like a weapon. "What are... Why are you..." She pointed to his crotch. "What..."

Jenna looked flushed and frightened. In any other situation or setting, his charm could sway her. Now, stripped to his skin, he experienced the full vulnerability his appearance displayed. For once, he wanted to cover his privates; a more confident Jeremy might have preened like a peacock before her, but seeing her tremble with her defenses on alert got to him. His lust for her lessened somewhat to a need to protect and assure her.

"What..." she repeated, softer this time.

"You said that already," he said, at a loss for a comeback.

"What is all this?" she demanded. "Why are you naked in my apartment?" She squinted at him. "Oh my God. Jeremy Vanderkellen?"

"In the flesh," he said with an awkward laugh. "More than most are used to seeing."

She shook her head. Any indication that she might have been fantasizing about him no longer existed in her now bewildered expression. "Is this a dream? How did you get in here? How do you even know where I live?"

"You invited me inside." When she vehemently denied this with another furious shake, Jeremy added, "Tell me this, do you hear any barking?"

She thought a moment, then her eyes went wide. "Oh, God. You killed a poor, defenseless dog?"

"I *am* a poor, defenseless dog, Jenna. Rather, I was. I'm supposed to be a *werewolf*." He drifted into the living room, drawn to the main window. Outside, the full moon was as round and bright as a communion wafer, yet Jeremy was unaffected. How could this be? Surely Alban's abilities couldn't defy wolf nature?

"What kind of bullshit are you trying to sell me?" Jenna cried, crossing an arm over her breasts as though finally realizing she had no clothes. "There's no such thing as werewolves. You're nuts. Get the hell out of here before I call the cops."

"No such thing, eh? Just like there's no such thing as elves, like the ones who took Dina to their world?" He saw Jenna's eyes widen in the dim of the room. "Admit it. You saw them slip through the fabric separating realities."

She shook her head, though he could tell by the confusion touching her features that her beliefs slowly shifted. "They *kidnapped* her," she insisted, though not as strongly as she had earlier that day. "It was a trick."

"It was *real*. I didn't have to be there to know the truth. And I am a werewolf."

"No such thing." Her growing doubt of her denial sounded in her voice.

"There *is*. I was the dog you brought into this house. You were arguing outside your door with a man in a blue shirt and jeans. I leaped up and bit his ass. Be honored, because I don't do that for everybody."

"You could have watched all of that from the distance," Jenna argued. "I wasn't really paying attention to who else was outside."

"'You sleep in the sun, you shit on the floor, and it's not your problem.' Those were your exact words to Schnookums, right?"

Jenna was hesitant, shocked, but belligerent. The spiked shoe that had hung loosely from her fingers was now pinned to her chest, heel outward. "If you're telling the truth, change back," she demanded. "Wolf out."

"I wouldn't do that if I could right now, Jenna. It would be too risky. Besides, I don't have control over my paranormal abilities at the moment."

"Because there's no such thing as paranormal abilities, or werewolves!"

"Just like a woman can't disappear into thin air?" Jeremy challenged, raising an eyebrow. When no retort came, he continued. "Just like a woman can't have an orgasm while sitting in a chair, untouched?"

It took a few seconds, but Jenna gaped. "That really happened? I...I thought that was a dream."

Jeremy shook his head. "And neither is this." He reached forward for her hand, relieved she didn't immediately jerk away. He placed it on his rapidly pounding heart. "Or this," he added, sliding it down his chest to where the tip of his growing cock tapped at his belly.

She surprised him by cuffing his shaft and testing its girth. "I'd have to be dreaming...or drunk. I should throw you out."

"Why don't you?"

She lifted a shoulder in a lazy shrug, then released his cock. "Maybe I liked what you did to me today. Maybe I want more."

"Why?" Jeremy asked. "To forget Dina? Or because it's what you really want?"

Jenna eyed him suspiciously. "If you're a werewolf, why were you a Chihuahua tonight?"

"I'm being taught a lesson, it seems." He gasped when Jenna grabbed him again playfully and tugged. "When the Head Wolf wants to get it across that somebody in his pack is a dog, he goes the extra mile. You didn't answer my question: Do you want more because you want me?"

Jenna slowly nodded. "I have to admit, I do. But you weren't going to help me find Dina," she said in accusation. "Maybe you *are* a dog."

"I told you before, I wouldn't know where to begin. If you stop for a second and look beyond your own place in this world, you'll be surprised to discover what's waiting."

He stepped just out of her reach, somewhat disappointed she didn't try to grab him again. Of course, he should expect her apprehension. The existence of fantastic creatures and other timelines was too much for a human to absorb in such a short time. Yet, Jeremy didn't have the luxury of a long orientation with her. If he wanted to be restored to his normal were-self, he had to help Jenna open her mind to these possibilities.

She cast her gaze to the floor, bringing her lips to a straight line. "She could have at least said good-bye," she said, her voice small.

"I'm sure she misses you. I can't see anybody not missing such a caring friend as you." When Jenna looked at him, he added, "Who else is searching for her? Her agent, any costars? I got the impression you took it upon yourself to find Dina."

"I loved her. *Love* her," she corrected herself. "She was practically family. I just want to know that she's okay."

"She is, I'm sure. If need be, I'll pull some strings and see if we can figure out where she is so you'll have some peace of mind."

Jenna nodded. She moved closer and allowed him to encircle her in his arms, presumably for comfort. He responded in kind when she looked down to realize, as if for the first time, that she too was naked. Jeremy relished the heated touch of her skin, her distended nipples so close yet barely brushing the feather soft hair on his chest.

"I'd like it if you could at least help me get a message to her, that I miss her."

"I'll do what I can, though I think I need your help more."

"How can I help?"

"I'm nothing without the support of my pack, I've discovered. Yet, even with them, I'm not complete without the love of a good woman. That's where you would come in."

"Come in, come often, I can dig it. What else have you learned, lone wolf?" she teased.

He nipped a kiss to her nose. "I've learned to see things from the ground up, for one," he said, walking backward with her to one couch. "I've learned how rather insignificant I am compared to the rest of the world."

"Mmm." Jenna eased herself between his parted knees, taking hold of his cock again as Jeremy lay back. "I suppose I could say these past few weeks have been a learning experience for me too."

"How so?"

She sank to the floor and knelt with her face at a level with Jeremy's hard-on. Quietly, yet with relish, she lapped up the length and kissed the tip before answering. "I do miss Dina. She was my friend and boss. And I suppose she was lonely, despite her fame. I didn't want to believe she would leave me willingly, but I should accept her decision to live in another dimension. If it exists, and it must if you're a werewolf."

"It's an alternate universe. We don't have to split hairs." Jeremy cringed at the bad joke.

Her tongue now ran south, swirling playfully around his sac for a few seconds. She lifted her upper body so that his cock bobbed between her breasts. "Whichever universe she's in, I hope she's happy. That's all she wanted. This universe, while I'm not the center of it, isn't too bad."

"I agree, I rather like some people here," Jeremy concurred. "I wouldn't mind having you centered on me, literally."

With a devilish smile, she leaned forward, bringing her hips up to meet his. He reached below to find that, thanks to the vibrator, she was already wet and willing. With one knee buried in the sofa and the opposite leg braced against the floor, Jenna raised her pelvis and pulled at the skin above her mound to expose her clit. Slowly, almost painfully, she rubbed her sensitive spot along his shaft, sending off a thousand sparks throughout his body. The sensation and accompanying image was too sexy, too intense to ignore. He felt ready to explode and hoped to whatever God existed that the woman would just ride him to sunrise. Suffice to say, it seemed conclusive that he was not going to change again.

She arched her back and closed her eyes, as though concentrating on the erotic rhythm of her movements. Her arms raised high, then her hands came back down to smooth her neck, décolletage, and nearly black nipples. He would have loved to sit up and take them into his mouth, but the view was too delicious to interrupt.

When she finally conceded to let his cock sink into her slick core, he shuddered from the friction. Tight, hot, and incredible. He grasped her hips and bucked upward into her. She countered with her own rocking motion, then bent low to take his mouth with hers. Tongues mating and their bodies pressed together, Jenna ground hard against him, speeding her pace so that orgasm for both was soon in coming. It happened first with such force that Jeremy had to tear away from her kiss to cry out. He seed shot upward into her womb, heating her channel and causing her to clamp around his cock to milk every last drop.

"God, that's so good," she groaned, and resumed her pace. With her parted nether lips still rubbing against him, her own climax followed in time. Her face, though pinched in orgasm and blurred by rapid movement, was still sexier than anything he'd ever seen.

When she finally floated back to him, they lay together motionless, their breathing synchronized. Jeremy kissed the top of her head and smiled as she snuggled closer. They should probably move to the bed, but he was beat. He imagined she'd fared no better.

"Well," he puffed, "here's to lessons learned."

"I don't know," Jenna said with mock skepticism. "I don't think I've been punished enough."

Jeremy chuckled. "We should all be so lucky to deserve such punishment."

Chapter Seven

Morning brought another unexpected visitor.

Jenna was in the kitchen making coffee when the bell rang. After a second round of "punishment" on the couch, the couple finally retired to the bedroom to sleep away the small hours. The rest fueled them plenty for morning lessons until Jeremy drifted off again. Looking forward to a lazy Saturday of sex and making acquaintance, she'd decided to let him snooze.

Her first thought was to ignore the summons. Only a religious witness would think to call so early on a weekend in this neighborhood, and she already owned a Bible, thank you. Yet, the knocking persisted, forcing her to turn away from the enticing aroma of ground hazelnut beans to expel whatever busybody had come to intrude.

Without checking the peephole, she ripped wide the door and snapped, "Go away, I'm Jewish." It was a lie, but she wasn't planning to pursue any friendships here.

Before her stood a bemused older gent who looked as if he had stepped off the cover of *Fortune 500* magazine. Despite the staid dress and manner, his eyes sparkled with the energy of someone half his age. "Well, so am I. Wasting a perfectly good Sabbath coming here, but there's not much I can do when duty calls." He stepped into the living room without being invited, toting a large paper bag. "I am Alban. I'm here for Jeremy."

"How did you know?" And realization quickly dawned. "Are you one of them?"

"I am."

"I didn't know werewolves could be Jewish. How is that possible?"

"Simple, because my mother was." With his hands pinned behind his back, Alban strolled the perimeter of the living room, taking in the knickknacks and art. "Good morning, Jeremy."

"Good morning."

She jumped at the sound of Jeremy's voice. Her heart pounded, then softened quickly as he emerged from the hall. A bath towel was fastened snugly around his waist, and his unkempt hair enhanced that handsome, disheveled look. Were it not for their guest, Jenna might have suggested a retreat to further mess up their appearances.

"Thank you for dressing," Alban told the other man dryly. "Here." The paper bag hit the floor at Jeremy's feet. "Fresh clothes for a new day. I won't presume to know what's been going on here. In fact, I can easily guess."

"Is it fair of me to presume you had some hand in it?" Jeremy asked. "Who else but a Head Wolf has the ability to change anybody *during* the full moon?"

Alban smiled and nodded. "It is a very rare gift, revealed by a specific genetic marker. Unfortunately for you, you don't possess it. I must admit, that is partly the reason I had to pass you over for promotion, son."

Jeremy appeared to concede to his elder's words, which confused Jenna. So this man was Jeremy's leader, not just an ordinary werewolf? "Promotion?" she asked. "You were supposed to lead the wolves?"

"Apparently not. I'm guessing Richard has this marker?" Jeremy queried.

Alban nodded again. "Had you been the model of good behavior, Jeremy, I'd still have to defer to him. It's not personal. It's for the good of the pack."

"Turning Jeremy into a Chihuahua was for the good of your pack too?" Jenna felt a bit angry at the notion. "Before I knew who he was, I saw that dog. Alone in the city, he could have been hurt."

"We wouldn't have allowed that to happen," Alban said soothingly, offering a placating gesture. "Jeremy can be irritating, yes, but he's family and I would never see him in danger. He had protection all along and would have been rescued if things got too rough."

"Protection?" Jeremy wrinkled his brows. "You don't mean Miss Wallace. The same woman who kicked me out of my own apartment?"

"What woman?" Was this jealousy panging her heart now? "Who's Miss Wallace?"

"Nobody you should be worked up over, love," Alban chuckled. "Just a very good, ah, *friend* of mine."

"I see." There was the twinkle in the old man's eye again. Jenna understood, despite the barrage of unfamiliar names.

"Really?" Jeremy sounded unconvinced. "If she was out to protect me, why put me in danger in the first place? I could have stayed out the night at home."

Alban scratched his chin, considering the theory. "Yes, and would you have learned anything? Would you have found the love needed to break the curse?" His expression sharpened. "*Did* you find the love?"

Jenna looked at Jeremy. The electricity sparked from their locked gaze warmed her inside and set her body to melt. She barely knew the man, yet felt so close to him. Genetic marker or no, she sensed his power and authority. He certainly had the confidence for it, if their initial meeting had been any indication.

"I think," Jenna said, "he found the right place."

Jeremy smiled.

"Good to know. I have just such a place, and I'm headed there now. A long night in the woods alone always leaves me yearning for it." Alban moved to leave, nonplussed by Jenna's sudden burst of laughter.

"I'll assume, if things go at this pace, you'll be your old self by the next moon," Alban was saying as he reached the door. He turned back for confirmation, and Jenna noted the surprise on the older man's face.

"To tell the truth, Alban, that doesn't concern me right now," he said. "If I have to be a lapdog for a while, fine. At least I don't have to vacate the city."

At this, he moved close and wrapped an arm around her waist. Jenna's heart danced at the contact. Was the werewolf magic doing this to her? She thought a moment, then studied Jeremy and saw no strange wriggling of his fingers. No, this rush of emotion came purely by Jeremy just being here for her.

The old man smiled. "It would appear you've learned more than I hoped," he said, and left.

"I have," Jeremy whispered softly into her ear. "I can't wait to learn more."

"Same here," Jenna murmured. "Do you think a human and a werewolf can live happily ever after in this reality?"

"If two elves from another reality can find true love with a television actress from this one, anything is possible. Now" -- he leaned down to nibble her neck -- "how about breakfast?"

"Sure," she said, pulling away, "but how about first we walk the dog?" She tugged Jeremy on a short walk down the hall to her bedroom.

Sweet Surprise

Sorry, babe, looks like you drew the short Popsicle stick again.

Josie shook the echo of phlegm-choked laughter from her mind. Always, she was stuck with this route. Always, the other drivers managed to arrange it so that only she made deliveries along what had been coined the Highway to Hell. Sierra Glade, while hardly reeking of the stench of brimstone, gave Josie the creeps. There was something peculiar, something so *Munsters* about the town that she could not quite discern, though the place looked like any other hamlet on her route. Her stomach roiled at the mere thought of going there again and again. She couldn't believe one tiny shop sold so much ice cream that she had to come so often.

Thankfully, this week's load was lighter than usual, and if Sweet Surprise had sufficient help in collecting their order, she could be out of town and on her way to the next stop within the hour.

She sighed with defeat as the truck rumbled past the patchwork sign welcoming her to Sierra Glade. Most hamlets on her delivery route had similar signs, bearing badges for the Knights of Columbus, the local Moose Lodge, and the Masons. Sierra Glade didn't seem fit to advertise any such civic organizations, taking care instead to inform newcomers that the town headquartered the International Elizabeth Montgomery Fan Club, the Sisters of Salem Local #420, and another club whose coat of arms depicted a sabre-toothed wolf devouring a bug-eyed weasel, or something. Josie never bothered to slow down to confirm; this time, as she always did, she focused on the road, and her job.

The sooner she got to Sweet Surprise, the sooner she could have their standing order of fifty vats of ice cream delivered. The sooner this light on the intersection of Bates and Transylvania changed—Josie snorted at the eerie appropriateness of the town's street names—the closer she would get to the store, to unload the ice cream, to hand the creepy lady owner her invoice, and get out of town.

Rather, though, than see any of that happening in the next thirty seconds, Josie was forced to idle the truck on the white line as a menagerie of Sierra Glade folk paraded across the street. They looked harmless and inconspicuous enough in jeans and T-shirts, blouses and long skirts, but something about the townsfolk bothered Josie. It wasn't something she could see or name outright; it seemed to her every native she encountered, every smile aimed in her direction, gave off an underlining, mischievous aura. It seemed as if the entire town was in on one grand in-joke, and she was the butt. A great big, J-Lo butt.

Josie felt silly enough in the uniform she had to wear—the pink blouse with Peter Pan collar, the pointed cap with the jingle bell on the end which flopped about her head like a deflated, tinkling breast. She didn't need the added anxiety this town contributed to her growing paranoia.

And she definitely didn't need this bozo in the puffy Jerry Seinfeld shirt and tight black pants planted in the middle of the road, facing the idled truck with a scowl and an exaggerated pirate's stance.

"What the...?"

The light turned green. He didn't budge. Josie scowled and tapped the horn. Clearly, he was a deaf bozo, too.

"Move, guy," she muttered.

She squinted past the glare cast through the windshield and got a good look at the tall blond, but the next curse died in her throat as her lips parted.

He was a *gorgeous* bozo. Josie took in the man's shoulder-length blond hair, lined with a few braided strands, sculpted cheeks and chin, and ocean blue eyes that seemed to pierce her soul.

They were doing something else to her, too. Josie squirmed in her seat as a growing want warmed her pussy and soaked her panties. Never before had a man prompted such a lustful reaction that quickly. Made sense, considering the sweaty, toothless drivers with whom she worked were the only men she saw on a daily basis.

Josie rolled down the driver's side window just as he rounded the steaming front grill, his fists still pinned to his hips. Was this how Yul Brynner used to walk, so formidable and masculine? Her fingers trembled as she gripped the door, and she immediately felt silly for her fear. What could this man possibly do to her, aside from causing her clit to explode with desire? He was well on the way to doing that, yet the serious look on his face told Josie that the man was not out for a pleasure stroll.

Despite the rush of desire she felt, she knew she was protected in the cab of the truck. Logically, since he was out of the way, she knew she should be pushing past the green light to make her delivery. Why did she remain idle?

Maybe she wanted another look, so he could finish the job, and she could orgasm? Then she could deliver the shipment, meet the creepy lady owner, yada-yada-yada. But, please, let the orgasm come first. It had been so long since Josie had experienced one that hadn't involved something made in Taiwan that required AA batteries.

She coughed as an exhaust cloud wafted upward. The stench of burning fuel nauseated her, but the pirate pedestrian appeared unaffected.

"You are to cease immediate the delivery of Dixie Belle Ice Cream," he demanded.

"What?" Who was this guy? Why did all the good-looking ones have to be nuttier than the vat of butter pecan cooling in the refrigerated truck?

He arched an eyebrow, and his lips twitched. Josie gunned the motor in protest. As annoyed as she was with this man, she was more annoyed with herself for imagining those same lips pursed around her clit and pulling it deep into his mouth. She was going to have to spend some quality time sitting on a vat of cherry vanilla to cool down her pussy when this confrontation ended.

"This is a Dixie Belle delivery truck, is it not?" His deep voice sent a ripple down Josie's back that circled her waist and shot upward, prickling her nipples. Surely now, she looked even more ridiculous in her uniform.

Josie straightened in her seat and steeled herself not to produce any more lustful thoughts. *Do your job*, she told herself, and put the truck into gear. She had ice cream to deliver.

When she turned back to the road, however, she

found a line of Sierra Glade folk—Sierra Gladettes, whatever they called themselves—blocking the crosswalk and crowded on both street corners, watching the exchange. The stoplight had cycled through a second time, yet no car horns sounded in protest. Everybody was watching the show, and Josie was the inadvertent star. She wouldn't be leaving Sierra Glade anytime soon.

Shit.

"Is this not," the man repeated slowly, as if addressing a child, "a Dixie Belle truck?"

"What's it to you?" Josie barked. So what if he was gorgeous, and so what if all Josie could think about was this puffy shirt guy pressing her against the cold truck panel and pounding his cock into her aching core, he was obviously a troublemaker...and *blind*. How could anyone with eyesight not see the gigantic Dixie Belle logo on the side of the truck? How could anyone not miss the image of the waif-like brunette pixie in gold short shorts and halter top, seductively licking a triple scoop cone of red, white, and blue creams? *Dixie Belle feeds America well* read the glittery red slogan underneath the company's soft-core mascot. Josie thought the image demeaning, and had to question the ethics behind using such a mascot to advertise to children, yet her opinion was in the minority. If she hated the logo so much, why not quit and drive for somebody else, she had been asked time and again.

Josie sighed and looked balefully at her captor. Why indeed? For all her grumbling about Dixie Belle, they were a good company, the leading brand of dairy dessert products in the region. The benefits and pay were too good to pass.

"You will cease delivery of this product immediately," the puffy shirt said.

It would appear that I already have. Josie rolled her eyes. He was gorgeous, but his demeanor was fast overlapping his more attractive qualities. Did he represent a competing brand? Dixie Belle had more than its share of detractors—the big player on the block usually did.

She smirked. "Are you Ben or Jerry?" She was pleased that she was able to disguise her lust with the sarcasm.

The blond stretched his lips into a smile that could have melted Sweet Surprise' entire standing order. "I am Lur," he said. Josie's own core melted as well. She could feel her pussy lips swell and throb with anticipation.

"Lur." She tested the word on her tongue. It was harsh and rough, likely as rough as the large hands now steepled at Lur's broad chest. Coupled with the devilish glint in his eyes, he struck a comical, movie villain pose.

Lur. Josie had not heard of such a brand name for dairy desserts. Regardless of who he was, and how prominent the bulge in his pants appeared, Josie could not let this charade continue. "Well, *Lur,*" she tested the harsh syllable that was his name, "I'm sorry, but I answer only to the Dixie Belle Corporation. Unless you have some kind of affidavit, or cease and desist order..." Or whatever it was that was needed to stop operations...Josie didn't know. She didn't care. She had her fun ogling the cute, crazy guy, but she had a job to do. She'd be nuttier than a prepackaged Dixie Belle Nutty Sundae Delight cone to want to hook up with anybody from here, anyway, even for a quickie.

Forget it, no point in bothering to keep talking. She reached for the gear shift, and grunted with growing exertion as she discovered it wouldn't budge. The stick protruding from the steering column felt as if it had been plunged into quick-dry cement. Josie pulled with all her strength, certain she would break it off.

"Come on," she cursed, hearing the stick crack.

Then the engine died on her. Josie cranked the key but wasn't even greeted with the requisite hum of a wheezing engine.

A loud *click* caught her attention and her head snapped back to the door. It had unlocked on its own. The truck didn't have power locks.

Lur remained still, but his hands were raised now, poised over his head, conducting the chaos to come. Josie didn't like the look on his face. The actual face, yes…

Ugh. It had been way too long since she had a good deep-dicking. She was supposed to be mad at this guy for stalling her, though she felt angrier that he wasn't stalling her in a more pleasurable way.

The door opened by itself, and as Josie attempted to reach for the handle she discovered she, too, couldn't budge.

"What the…?" She was frozen, able only to turn her head and witness her fate. This man, this…Lur, had put some kind of spell on her. What else could explain this? What else could explain the mild indifference of the gathering crowd of onlookers, all of whom had clearly chosen to watch instead of help? *Come on*, Josie silently willed the bystanders. *I'm the ice cream lady, I'm the good guy.* She knew there was something about this town, these people. They were all indifferent to strangers, or so bored with their lives that they felt they had to be apathetic in order to be entertained. Or, maybe this was some kind of protest against big corporations edging into little towns. That explained the lack of Starbucks and Panera Bread.

She gasped as Lur eyed her with delicious mischief, the way a dieter off the wagon might eye a triple fudge parfait. Josie could feel her own blood sugar skyrocket into her brain; she was floating inside her skin, wanting an anchor, wanting to be boarded by this pirate.

Arrrr!

It appeared she would soon get that wish. Lur's hands lowered and his fingers splayed in her direction, well-timed with a rumbling sensation that started in her abdomen and spread through her limbs and buttocks. The overall effect was frightening, but the vibrations caused her pussy to melt, and that feeling was too delightful to protest. She tried to scream, but her protest spilled forth instead into a pleasured moan.

The seatbelt came free, and the strap disentangled itself from her body. The hat slipped from her head and tinkled sadly to the floor. Pink pearl buttons popped free from her blouse, revealing lacy white cups concealing ample, creamy breasts. Slowly her body moved, pushed by an invisible force across the bench seat to the other side of the spacious cab. Josie was pressed against the cold steel of the opposite door as Lur leaped forward into the cab and waved his hands once again.

The door slammed shut behind him, the locks engaged, the dome light extinguished. Josie's gaze panned the cab windows. All eyes were upon them, faces without emotion, watching and waiting…

Lur produced a cell phone from an unseen pocket and dialed three numbers.

"I am Lur," he announced in that sexy, sundae-melting voice. "I've taken a hostage."

* * * * *

"Say what?"

Lur smiled. "What," he said.

Josie shook her head. It was the only thing she could still do, as Lur's magical hold had yet to loosen. "It's an expression," she sighed. "It means say it again."

"It again." Lur leaned back against the driver door and propped a booted foot on the bench. The opposite knee wavered lazily back forth under the steering column. Every now and again Josie could catch a glimpse of an impressive bulge tenting the crotch of Lur's pants.

She blew away a strand of hair brushing across her nose, making it itch. As soon as she was free of this unseen bondage, she would knee this bozo in the groin. Never mind that she wouldn't have minded fondling it first. "Who were you calling just now?"

"Why, the media," Lur said innocently. "Standard procedure when taking a hostage."

The media had one central number? Josie wasn't

buying it. "Of course, and what was that about taking me as a hostage again?" she asked through gritted teeth.

"Ah, yes." Lur chuckled and tapped idly at the wheel. "That is correct. You are to remain my hostage until the Dixie Belle Corporation agrees to my demands. I apologize it must come to this, but your employers have not been very cooperative. Yes," he stretched and gave Josie a marvelous view of fabric stretched over taut arm and chest muscles, "once Dixie Belle agrees to cease use of the name and logo you will be free."

Oh, please. "Look, buddy, it didn't work with Disney and it's not going to work with some small time operator like you." Josie knew her bravado might have had more impact were she not directing this statement at Lur's crotch, which was anything but small time. She silently cursed her raging hormones and glanced out the window. Why wasn't anybody helping? Why were people positioning lawn chairs among the now still traffic?

Why wasn't Lur making a move?

"What's your beef with Dixie Belle, anyway?"

"Their improper and unauthorized use of my sister's name and likeness," Lur said evenly. He appeared to be sizing the interior of the cab, planning something.

"Your sister?"

"Dixie Belle. My sister, a faerie."

Josie's eyes widened. Nuttier than a slice of Dixie Belle Carrot Cake Surprise Ice Cream Torte, this man was. "Your sister is a fairy," she said, incredulous.

"And she's also lactose tolerant." Lur pinched the

bridge of his nose. "Nor does she dress like a two-bit whore, as your company implies in its advertising. That's what makes this whole thing all the more frustrating."

"A real fairy? Wings, the tinkling bells, the fairy dust and all that?"

"No." Lur rolled his eyes. "*Faerie*. She is fay, from Faerie," he said, and spelled it out for Josie. "We are a race of beings more gifted and culturally enhanced than you humans."

"Excuse me?" Josie raised an eyebrow, but she still couldn't move her hands. "You can't just make a blanket statement like that. I mean, humans are gifted and culturally enhanced, too." Was she really having this conversation? "Look at all our technological advancements. We have the Internet, we cure diseases...look at this truck! Two hundred years ago I couldn't ferry ice cream in an ox cart and get it to people still frozen. Let the faeries top that!"

"You also have reality shows and spoiled, attention-getting heiresses." Lur rolled his eyes. "I'd say two steps back for every leap forward."

Josie had no response to that; Lur did have a point.

All of a sudden, however, another issue crossed her mind. "Uh," she tried to shift and was still unnerved to be frozen, "okay, you 'called the media' and all, but how does loosening my blouse fit into your plan?" She willed the blouse to refasten itself, and cursed her body for succumbing to her urges. Josie tried to remain defiant, but it seemed difficult to have much credibility when her nipples threatened to poke through her bra.

Lur chuckled. "You challenge the fay folk to top your progress of refrigerated delivery trucks and spam e-mail, I say fair enough." He waved a hand in circular motion. Josie watched in awe as the back panel of the cab rippled, as if turned into liquid, then gasped as Lur stuck his hand through the truck. Seconds later he plucked a pint of ice cream meant for another delivery and studied the label.

"Did you just put your hand through the truck?" Josie cried.

Lur ignored the question. "Cherry Delight, my favorite," he said with a tinge of sarcasm, and tore off the lid. "One thing your company manages to do well."

"What the..." Josie looked at the back panel. It was solid again. She looked back at Lur. "How did you...? How?"

"It would appear the fay folk spent the centuries perfecting our own advances instead of developing television shows that feature people eating bugs for cash prizes. One thing we do well," he held up the pint, "is magic."

"Really? What else?" Josie looked around the cab. The windows were fogging.

And before she realized it, another wave of Lur's hand sent her clothes to the floor with her hat. She was naked, and still, and completely aroused. Every nerve ending stood to attention, ready to comply to this Faerie's command.

"The other thing we do well," Lur supplied with a wicked grin, "is lovemaking."

* * * * *

Yes!
What, no!
Well...

By no will of her own, Josie's wrists came together, as if bound by invisible cuffs, and were raised above her head so that they were pinned against the roof of the cab. Her breasts bobbed slightly, her nipples tightened with anticipation. She watched Lur trace the rim of the opened ice cream carton. Was he planning to slather her nude body with Dixie Belle Cherry Delight and lick away every last, milky drop? Was he thinking instead he would turn his cock into an ice cream pop and urge her to quit her diet?

Whatever he intended, why was he taking so damn long doing it?

The temperature in the cab had dropped, as indicated by a myriad of goose pimples covering her body. Lur, however, looked comfortable in his pseudo-pirate costume, as much as he did eyeing Josie's body with approval.

"Why are you doing this?" Josie wanted to know, her voice a whimper.

Lur plunged a finger into the cream and scooped a dollop, studying it before sucking it off his finger. "A Faerie's got to be entertained somehow while waiting for his demands to be met," he said finally. "If, as you say, Dixie Belle is inflexible in negotiations, I plan to be here a while, as should you. And I don't see a television anywhere in here to watch, not that I'd care to see who gets voted off an elevator, or whatnot."

"No, I meant why are you doing this, *making me wait*? Why aren't you fucking me?"

Josie wanted to shrink back into the bench seat and disappear, fade away into a puff of cold air. She couldn't believe she had said that out loud, to a stranger, while bound naked in her own delivery truck. Truth be told, however, the cold hardly affected her pussy, which felt on fire for this man. It amazed her how much she wanted this man, her captor, a man she should be cursing with every breath. She wanted to sheath this man, this Faerie, in her hungry, throbbing core, and feel him pulse into her until the truck's shocks exploded. She wanted to block out the cold air, the controversy of infringed copyright, the whirr of helicopters overhead...

Helicopters?

She squinted past the veneer of fog covering the windshield. Great, the media had arrived. Josie couldn't discern any call letters, but it was a sure bet WSGL Action News was hovering overhead, panning close for a glimpse of her pink-tipped breasts and shaved pussy. Kidnapped ice cream delivery driver gets a double scoop surprise, film at eleven.

Right. She hadn't been offered a tiny sample spoon yet.

A tingling sensation coursed through her veins, and Josie felt her body give. Save for the pinned wrists, she could move again. She writhed in place and spread her legs to get the blood circulating again. That was her excuse, anyway. She really wanted to show this gorgeous Faerie what he was missing by stalling. She wanted him to see her swollen labia, her glistening slit, and tempt him away from the ice cream for a taste of Josie Delight.

Lur flashed her another wicked smile. "Comfortable?"

Josie's answer was to nudge Lur's thigh with a brightly-painted, pointed toe. She stroked upward until she hit cock, then stroked some more.

"I will say this," Lur said, "you're a very cooperative hostage." He scooped another bite of ice cream and topped each toe, then cupped Josie's heel in hand and sucked each digit clean. "A delicious one as well."

"Always willing to take one for the team," Josie murmured, so long as the team wasn't comprised of her chucklehead co-workers. "So you know, some parts taste better than others."

"We'll see about that." Out came the chirping cell phone and Lur spoke in a clipped tone. "Any word yet?" he barked into the receiver, then smiled. "Good. I'll wait."

Josie blinked, surprised to see that the phone had suddenly turned into a can of maraschino cherries. How did that happen? "Like magic," she whispered.

"Like?" Lur tut-tutted, shaking his head. "My dear, you have a lot to learn about being a hostage. This *is* magic. As is this." A snap of the fingers popped an aerosol can of whipped cream into his other hand.

Yummy. Josie thanked the stars she had no dairy allergies.

Lur crawled closer to Julie, shaking the whipped cream can. The loud sucking sound absorbed the sound of their heavy breathing as Lur covered each of Josie's breasts with the cream, creating two spiraled pyramids. He topped each mound with a cherry, then leaned back to admire his handiwork.

Good enough to eat. Yet Josie wondered why Lur wasn't indulging. "Don't tell me you're lactose intolerant, too."

"No, just think I'd like to start with something sweeter." Lur set the pint between Josie's legs and barely brushed the carton against her parted pussy lips. The chilled sensation was delightful, but did nothing to suppress her desire. When Lur tipped the carton toward her and let a stream of melted ice cream drip down her pussy, she wanted to cry. Pure torture this was, no way to treat a prisoner. Amnesty International would hear about this, to say nothing of the dairy board.

Finally Lur set the pint on the dashboard and dipped his head low. One broad stroke of the tongue lapped up most of the cream, and Lur licked his lips. "Yes," he growled, "very sweet."

He bent down again and, parting Josie's cleft with two cold fingertips, suckled her pussy. Josie writhed in his oral hold, moaning with every touch of his tongue to her labia. When his lips pursed around her clit and pulled slightly she thought she would go mad. To think this morning she had been angry to draw the short Popsicle stick...if the guys in dispatch only knew. The stick she saw bulging in Lur's pants was anything but.

"Yes," Lur kissed into her pussy, "you're being very cooperative. I think negotiations are going to go very well."

"Yes," Josie sighed, then gasped as Lur's tongue swirled around her clit in rapid circles. A slow burn smoldered in her core, building as the pressure to her clit increased, until finally Josie sensed an eruption was imminent.

As the first orgasm hit Josie bucked her hips forward, but Lur stayed with her. He dipped lower to lap up her pussy juice and teased her slit with a few broad licks. Never before had Josie felt such a sugar rush.

Lur then kissed a trail up Josie's quivering abdomen. "You will cease delivery of Dixie Belle Ice Cream to Sierra Glade."

"Yes."

His mouth took possession of one breast, but not before he sucked in the cherry. The sensation tickled her, delighted her, made Josie wish Lur had drawn whipped cream trails over other parts of her body and created an edible road map to devour. She'd have no qualms about taking that kind of trip.

His tongue teased that cream-covered nipple, bit lightly and sucked it in deep before releasing it with a light *pop*. "Your company will cease the use of the Dixie Belle name and logo bearing any likeness to the real Dixie Belle."

"Yes," Josie moaned. She had no idea how she could make that happen, but if Lur kept going she'd find a way. She'd infiltrate the unions, rally the workers to a slowdown, chain herself to the CEO's desk in protest...so long as Lur. Did. Not. Stop.

He feasted on the other breast. "Your company will issue a written apology to Dixie Belle for sullying her image."

"Yes." Sullying was bad. Soooo bad.

Josie looked down the length of Lur's body.

Somewhere in the course of Lur's dessert his puffy shirt and pants had disappeared, granting her full view of rippled muscles taut under smooth, tanned skin. Smoother than a butterscotch malt, leaner than a low-carb fruit pop. Infinitely more delicious.

The tip of his bulging cock bobbed right at the entrance to her channel, teasing her pussy lips and raising her desire. She felt ready to melt into a puddle.

Lur cuffed his cock in one hand and tweaked her nipple with the other. He guided his cock closer to her, and traced the edge of her slippery core. "You will comply with all of my demands," he ordered softly.

"I will."

He braced one knee against the bench seat and eased slowly insider her. Josie delighted in the new sensation, the way his engorged cock filled her. She watched as he slowly disappeared inside her, and marveled at the realization of it. Let Dixie Belle hem and haw in their corporate offices, she could wait.

Lur pumped in and out of her pussy, two short thrusts followed by one longer one. "And, after your superiors have finally seen reason and surrendered what is rightfully ours..."

He pivoted his hips. Josie felt the change in thrust clear to her toes. *Yes...*

"...you will get rid of that ridiculous, stereotypical fairy uniform..." A kiss on the breastbone, then a series of lighter brushes across her jaw. Another orgasm bubbled deep within her.

Yes...

"...and come work for me." Lur punctuated this

final order with one long, hard thrust, so deep Josie thought Lur might tear through her. Instead she shuddered as the next orgasm crashed over her, timed with a bellowing roar from her partner, and she thrashed back into the passenger side window, not feeling a thing.

"Yes!" she cried. *Yes! Yes! Yes...*

What?

"What?" she echoed on the trip back to Earth. The cab was spinning. Condensation streaked the windows around them, creating long, crooked fingers through which Josie spied many cheering faces and applauding hands. Good night, had they just received a standing ovation? The sound of choppers returned in full force now as Josie realized where she was, and what she had been doing.

She had just fucked a stranger in her truck...in the middle of town...a stranger who now ostensibly was her boss.

She felt a tingling in her hands, and discovered the invisible bond was gone. Josie rubbed her wrists and tried to focus on the panting, naked man now reclining against the opposite window. "You want me to what now?" she gasped, dizzy.

Lur held up a finger as a familiar chime vibrated in the air. His cell phone materialized in hand. "Yes," he answered curtly, and smiled. "Excellent," he drawled, "we'll see you in Faerie anon.

"Your former employers have acquiesced," he informed Josie as he righted himself on the bench. Turning the key that had given her problems, Lur easily turned over the engine and set the truck to idle. "We have regained control of my sister's name and image, and you," he winked, "have a new job."

"I do?" So much for giving Dixie Belle, or whatever they would be called now, two weeks' notice. "Doing what?"

Lur put the truck in drive and eased through the parting crowd. Amazing how nobody had protested the traffic jam, and how quickly the lawn chairs and news vans and choppers had disappeared. Life in Sierra Glade had returned to its normal, creepy self. "Supervising the delivery of our frozen desserts, of course," he said. "Overseeing trucks to outlets all over Faerie and beyond and making sure stores receive their shipments of Dixie Belle."

"Dixie Belle? So this was all about regaining your sister's name to sell your own ice cream? I thought she was lactose intolerant."

"It's all soy-based." Lur waggled his eyebrows. "Less fat, better for you."

Josie noticed they had turned a corner, and she buckled up quickly. She felt weird being naked in a moving truck, but at least a Sierra Glade cop could cite her for a seatbelt violation. "Yeah, but you can still gain weight with non-dairy desserts."

"Not in Faerie," Lur smiled. "We have ways of burning calories."

And Josie's skin prickled again, though the cab was much warmer. "I see," she said, "and will we be burning many calories together in the future."

In the distance a large, swirling portal on the intersection of Transylvania and Mockingbird opened to reveal the road to what Josie figured had to be Faerie. Lur aimed in the truck in that direction as his hand came off the gear shift to caress her thigh.

"But of course," he said. "One of the many fringe benefits of working for Dixie Belle."

Josie smiled. Unlimited sixty-nine in lieu of a 401K suited her just fine.

Sugar on Top

Chapter One

Melina Munroe swept through the entrance of the Sweet Surprise ice cream parlor with a confident air that befit such a prominent citizen of Sierra Glade. Tiny bells attached to the hem of her flowing, batik-patterned cape tinkled a disjointed tune with her every step. She turned heads—disembodied and otherwise—as she breezed past a line of booths to the last one in the far corner.

A dismissive wave toward the front counter was her only greeting to her close friend, the shop's owner. "Andora, my usual, but no heavy cream this time," she barked. She didn't bother to turn back and acknowledge the ice cream parlor's owner. "I need to lay off the dairy for a while. It's given me so much mucus I'm coughing up seven shades of green these days."

All around the parlor, spoons clattered quietly to plates and bowls, desserts uneaten as a collective unease spoiled appetite after appetite in the otherwise busy parlor.

Melina, her focus still on the back booth, slid into the bench facing the wall and set down her heavy handbag. A tiny gecko attempted escape but the woman eased it back into the bag's depths.

"Good morning, Sugar," Melina said blandly, and maintained her poker face when a quiet "Shit!" cut the air before her.

"How did you know I was here?" demanded Sugar Pernell's detached voice.

Nobody knew Sugar was in the shop this morning; at least, that had been Sugar's assumption. She slipped through the door behind a visible faerie couple and paced the floor for much of the morning. She avoided bodily contact and listened for any juicy bits that she might incorporate into her next gossip column for the *Sierra Glade Snitch*. After a short while, she grew tired and took the far, vacant bench. Though business at Sweet Surprise was active, nobody else approached the booth, until Melina came storming in the diner.

As one who could render herself invisible at will, the job suited Sugar perfectly. The paper's publisher should have been happy to see her, or rather *not* see her, working.

Melina, however, was not smiling. She clicked her tongue. "Child," she admonished. "Surely you should know that the hallmarks of being a good, investigative reporter are to be observant, and *discreet*. How could you think that nobody coming to the back of this shop, presumably to use the restrooms or play a song on the jukebox, *wouldn't* see the obvious impression on the bench seat that your invisible ass is making?"

Sugar looked down and sighed. When invisible, she couldn't see her own body, either. She could, however, see the rounded indentation that gave her away.

"Sugar?" Melina sang, and barely nodded as Andora set down her mug with a smirk in Sugar's direction. "Get any good gossip today?"

Sugar stayed silent. She hadn't, and it appeared Melina didn't need to be told.

"Have you noticed, too, the bare footprints still on the floor?"

Sugar followed Melina's broad gesture toward the spacious dining area, and grimaced. *Damn it.* She'd forgotten to wipe her feet before entering. Tiny footprints, faded but clearly visible, remained in wavy circular patterns.

Melina batted at a tiny blue envelope until the sweetener inside clumped at one end. "Honestly, child," she sniffed, "I don't see the advantage of invisibility if you're going to be so sloppy. *Everybody* knows you're here. The reason you don't have anything for your column is because nobody here is that stupid to open his mouth."

"Fuck," Sugar muttered.

"Believe me, I'd rather be doing that than sitting here with you," Melina muttered. "I wouldn't be, either, if Andora hadn't called. Well, you might as well show yourself. Won't do you any good to sneak away. I can smell your perfume."

"I can't," Sugar said, her voice urgent. "Show myself, that is."

Melina looked at her with a raised brow, then nodded. "Of course, I forgot," she said.

"Of course," Sugar mimicked. She was naked, as it was the only way she could go about unseen. Her ability to render herself invisible didn't transfer to clothes, always a sore spot with Sugar. This morning was particularly cool—the shop's air conditioning seemed to be turned to high, and Sugar's nipples stood achingly at attention. Her skin suffered a near-perpetual prickled state.

Melina simply unhooked the silver clasp at her throat and pulled off her cape, the bells chiming in unison. She tossed it across the bench, and Sugar took shape as the fabric draped over her body. Sugar could see easily through the gauzy cape and wondered how much it would hide. As it was, nobody in the shop appeared surprised to see her emerge as she righted the cape around her nude form.

"Much better." Melina smiled, sipped from her mug, then folded her arms on the table. "I like to look a person in the eye before I fire her."

"Melina..." Sugar cried, further protests muted by Melina's scowl.

"Sugar, you're not giving me much of a choice here. Your gossip column isn't as good as it used to be, it's losing readership, and this slapshod manner of finding new material is clearly hurting you. I won't even tell you the results of the *Snitch*'s latest readers' poll."

"That bad?" Sugar said, meek. At the next booth, a waitress set down an enormous hot fudge sundae for a pair of shape-shifters to split. The aroma of warm chocolate and fresh fruit should have been pleasing, but Sugar's empty stomach roiled.

"Let's put it this way," Melina said. "Fifty percent of the readers want you replaced with *Beetle Bailey*, the other fifty want you permanently tattooed in neon ink so they can see you coming."

Sugar sank into the bench. To think, not three months ago these same readers praised her column for dishing Sierra Glade's dirt.

"I've opted instead," Melina was saying, "to give your column space to Winkle."

"Winkle? That conniving fairy?"

"Now, Sugar. That was just a phase in college, so he says. And I can't help his tastes in clothing."

Sugar shook her head wearily. She wasn't in the mood for jokes. Winkle was, literally, a fairy. His extremely short stature, coupled by a strong pair of wings, had made him an asset at the *Snitch* as a roving reporter — to procure gossip on the sly wouldn't be a problem for him.

Sugar had known for a while, too, that Winkle wanted his own column, and wondered how he managed to talk Melina into it. She wouldn't be surprised to hear later that those wispy wings affixed to Winkle's back could do more than fly. Fly Melina to the moon with a few swats to her clit, more than likely.

"Melina, please, give me one more chance," Sugar begged, and pulled the cape tighter around her body. The thin drape did little to keep her warm; she could feel her nipples poking through the fabric. "I know I haven't been at top form of late, but what if..."

She stopped as the bell at the front door signaled the entrance of a dark, handsome gentleman in a white turtleneck and charcoal pants. Warner Doctorow brushed fallen bangs from his forehead and scanned the breadth of the ice cream parlor before his piercing golden gaze settled on Andora. Smiling, he approached the shop's owner and greeted her with a friendly smile and handshake.

Oh, but he was gorgeous, and one of the most eligible bachelors in Sierra Glade now that Anton Drake was to be married.

"What if," Sugar repeated, her eye fixed on Warner, "I got you the scoop of the year?"

Melina stirred another packet of sweetener in her mug. "We already have somebody covering the Sweet Surprise Spectacular," she said, "and there's really not much gossip attached to that event."

"I don't mean a *literal* scoop, Melina. Warner Doctorow is hosting Anton's bachelor party tomorrow night. It's supposed to be top secret, but everybody knows about it. They just don't know what's going to happen. If I could just get inside..."

Melina looked up and turned, matching Sugar's gaze to the handsome gentleman now following Andora to the kitchen. "I see," she said, now smiling at Sugar. "Though, looking at you now, you'd probably rather have Warner inside of you."

Sugar rolled her eyes and didn't give Melina the satisfaction of flaunting her observational skills. "If I deliver details of the party, can I keep my column?"

"Yes," Melina said, firm. "And, to be safe, you'd better give me the cape back."

Sugar grinned and willed her body to fade. Her milk white skin, slender fingers, and long red hair dissolved into nothing.

"Seriously," Melina said. "The way you look at Warner, you're probably already about to come, and I don't want you getting it on my cape. She snatched back the jingling fabric. "And try not to drip on the floor."

Chapter Two

"Andora, it's beautiful."

Hands clasped behind his back, Warner admired the wide tower of frosted cake layers before him, arranged to form a jagged pyramid ringed in ribbons and flowers. Blue and white, to match the bride's wedding colors. Ceramic bridal figurines perched arm in arm on the topmost layer. Little did they know this cake would be used for an entirely different ceremony.

Yes, Warner decided, Andora had outdone herself with this culinary masterpiece. Such a shame, though, that Anton's intended would never see this majestic confection. Nor, for that matter, would she ever know of the willowy blonde Faerie that Warner hired to pop out of the cake and give Anton Drake a lap dance guaranteed to send his cock exploding through his jeans. That would teach his best friend to leave behind his friends and partying lifestyle to get married, Warner mused with a wicked smile.

His finger barely brushed against the frosting; he didn't wish to mar Andora's handiwork. The cake looked so beautiful, he almost felt saddened to know it would be demolished at Anton's bachelor party. Of course, the hope that much of the confection would be smeared on and eaten off a nude Faerie's body assuaged the guilt...all for a good cause.

"I like the ribbons around each layer." He indicated the shiny fabric, waving the finger as a conductor might, tracing the ribbon's path. "How do you get them to stay up like that?"

"Marzipan," Andora said.

Warner nodded. He knew nothing of cake decorating, but Andora's authoritative tone told him not to challenge her expertise. "Fascinating," he said. "It's a very versatile confection."

Andora laughed. "You misunderstand me, Warner. The *ribbon* is marzipan. The flowers, too. Everything on that cake is edible, even the figurines."

"Really?" Warner liked the sound of that. "And...the other feature we mentioned?"

Though a tall woman, Andora tilted her head back a bit to look up at him. Warner could feel her knowing gaze study him. There wasn't much one could put past a Sierra Glade sorceress. "The cake is completely hollow inside, and the bottom layer has a spell attached. This table is enchanted, too, so your gal can slip through the wood surface into the cake without causing a structural breach. You don't have to touch a thing." She handed him a white tube. "If any the flowers get messed up, use this tube of softened marzipan to fix them. I'll hazard a guess that you're, ah, *friend* will know what to do once she's in the cake?"

"Indeed she will." Warner felt the stirrings of an erection teasing him at the thought of it. Once the lovely Fae Falona was secured inside the cake, then it would be *completely* edible. He was certainly going to enjoy licking sugar frosting off her taut breasts and belly as she writhed on his lap. The best parts, of course, would be saved for the groom.

"And I'll hazard *another* guess," Andora's tone darkened, "that this party you're throwing for my cousin won't result in anything that will threaten his wedding? Cindy's a nice girl, and I don't want her getting hurt."

"I can assure you I will do my best to deliver Anton to the altar unharmed...and unspoiled. It's my sworn duty as best man."

"I hear this bachelor party is supposed to be wildest shindig Sierra Glade's seen since the Dixie Belle people built that gigantic hot fudge sundae in the town square, to celebrate getting their name back." Andora smirked, her gaze fixed on a faraway point. "Then hosted an orgy in it."

"Really?" Warner feigned innocence, but couldn't resist a smile. He remembered the orgy well, and was certain he still had candy sprinkles stuck in places where sprinkles shouldn't be.

Anton's party would be wild, yes, but not to that extent. Select guests were coming by invitation only, no exceptions. How often those select guests would *come*, was anybody's guess.

"We're just going to eat cake and play Texas Hold 'Em all night," he said.

"And the naked Faerie, Miss Falona? Is she on the menu?"

"Somebody has to deal the cards, Andora."

Andora frowned. "Yes, well, hear this, Mr. Best Man. Cindy believes *Anton* is the best man around. Let's keep him that way, eh? And speaking of delivering..."

Warner already had out his checkbook. He added an extra zero to the fee in hopes of buying Andora's silence, as she was the only other person to know about the cake's secret. "No worries. My SUV is waiting outside. I've had a special charm set on the house so there are no unexpected guests, particularly the media. This is a private affair, and I'm afraid your deliverymen won't make it very far if they try." He paused, then added, "Did you hear something?"

"Just you talking," she said. "You know, before I took on this project, I hadn't realized how anal you werewolves can be." Andora took the check, but didn't register any emotion upon seeing her generous tip. "I'll have to remember that the next time one of *your* kind comes in here with a special order."

Warner leaned in close, buzzing her ear with a low-throated moan. He knew the lovely shopkeeper to be married now, but she was still as delectable as any dessert served under her roof. "The devil's in the details, my dear. And I *love* giving anal." His gaze panned down her scoop-necked blouse and took in her generous breasts. "What is that lovely perfume you're wearing?"

"Marizpan."

"You know, love, if you'd give me a chance..."

Andora playfully pushed Warner away. "There aren't enough zeroes in your bank account for that, wolfie. Try not to get indigestion tonight, eh?"

Chapter Three

Ugh! Was Warner taking the shortcut through the quarry or purposely hitting every pothole in the street for sport?

Sugar huddled inside the hollow cake, her knees tucked under her chin, her arms wrapped around her crossed legs. It was a very uncomfortable position, and the surrounding aroma of sugar and cake was overwhelming, but Sugar didn't dare move. The space was quite narrow; large enough for the petite Fae Falona, perhaps, but not so much for a taller gal like herself.

That Warner's SUV seemed to be rolling and bumping over a miles-long path of gravel did little to ease the trek to his house. Sugar bounced along with the cake in the back, ducking her head and trying not to dent the cake from the inner chamber. *Slow down*, she admonished the werewolf silently.

One would think a wealthy werewolf like Warner Doctorow could afford to buy good shocks. The party wasn't until tomorrow night, what was the rush?

Sugar sighed. Her back ached, her neck ached, and her butt was asleep. It was dark inside the hollow dessert, and she felt short of breath. She wanted to sneeze, but didn't dare do anything to attract attention to herself. Werewolves had a keen sense of hearing and smell, and Sugar wondered if Warner noticed her perfume as she slipped, invisible, through Andora's kitchen into the cake per the baker's instructions. She feared being caught when it appears he'd heard her shuffling around.

She felt grateful to get this far, and would feel

much better once the cake issue settled. At the first free moment, she would slip away unnoticed, and hide out somewhere in Warner's behemoth mansion until the party hit full swing.

If only she could move about right now, and ease the aching in her body. Thinking of Warner enhanced the feelings as thoughts of his strong hands massaging away the numbness surfaced. She imagined his hands rubbing away the kinks in her neck and shoulders, then dipping low to play with her labial folds and clit. What she could feel of her thighs grew moist with her quiet excitement.

Ugh. She had to get out of this cake now before the bottom layer soaked up too much of her juice. Sugar doubted this cake was meant to be actually eaten, but surely Warner would detect *that* in the first bite if he did.

She tapped the cake floor with a toe, and burrowed her foot deeper into the moist, edible sponge until she hit...table.

Shit. Everything stood solid now, and she remained trapped. Had she voided the charm after slipping inside?

Then it hit Sugar as her head raised slowly and she peered into the inky black in search for a light that couldn't be seen...unless she did one thing first. The spell placed on the cake was one-way, meaning that the only way out would be to jump out of the cake.

As meant to be the plan for Fae Falona at Anton's bachelor party, before a horde of drunken, horny werewolves, vampires, and other assorted menfolk. Every girl's dream.

How could she escape without blowing her cover, and without destroying the cake? Sugar knew no counter spells, none that involved bakery goods, anyway. Worst case scenario would have her stuck here for a whole day, then squeezed inside the cake with a half-naked faerie stripper. Granted, Warner might not object to *that*, but once he sobered and learned of her true intent...

Sugar exhaled slowly, feeling dizzy. How could she survive in here until tomorrow night without going insane, and not eating her way to freedom?

* * * * *

Warner couldn't get home quickly enough. The ache of impending change tingled his every nerve. The full moon wasn't expected for hours, yet Warner felt the wolf inside him jockeying for premature release. His gums were sore, a precursor to the monthly return of his fangs, and as he turned the steering wheel sharply to plow his SUV into his home garage he noticed the beginning of the telltale extension of his fingernails.

He sighed. His time of the month.

Well, best to have the wolf come out early, he decided, if it guaranteed a premature exit. He silently cursed his best friend for his hasty engagement, then scheduling the wedding for the day after tomorrow, consequently leaving Warner with such a short window for hosting this party. He had intended for Anton's last night as a free man to be wild, but the added unpredictability of a werewolf running amok among the inebriated was not in the plans. He didn't want to be let loose, as was his wont in the past. He needed to remain close to home to ensure the success of Anton's party. To say nothing of discretion.

There were methods, of course, of curbing the transformation, even postponing it entirely until the next full moon. A delicious smile split Warner's face as his sport utility vehicle eased to a stop inside his spacious garage. Two things, in particular, worked best: sex and food, and he was well-prepared for this month's eventuality. The pantry was overstuffed with party snacks and other favorite treats, in the event a binge became necessary to keep the wolf from emerging.

And, if that didn't work...

Warner chuckled as the garage door lowered behind him. He killed the engine and flipped open his cell phone. The lovely Fae Falona picked up on the second ring.

"That wasn't part of the deal," she told him after hearing his proposal. To her credit, however, Falona didn't sound put off by Warner's invitation.

"I'm not suggesting you prostitute yourself, my dear. I hired you to jump out of the cake, only," Warner purred seductively. "Consider everything else that happens a fringe benefit." How he'd like to see her dripping in fringe, then shedding it for a marathon fuck in his king-sized bed.

Falona giggled. "I've always wanted to fuck a werewolf in transition, but you never call when it happens."

"Well, now's your chance. The closer to the full moon, the better the sex," Warner drawled. He shifted in his seat to better allow his cock to harden and expand in his pants. He stroked the shaft lightly over the fabric seam and pictured Falona's long, blonde hair draped over his thighs as she perched between them for better oral access.

"You fuck a werewolf, you transcend doggie style. I'm talking about hanging from the ceiling, limbs twisted like a master yogi." He flicked his tongue against his growing fangs. The ladies loved especially how they scraped lightly against skin as he sucked their clits. "You'd be doing me a great service by aiding in certain, ah, preventative measures, *and* you get the experience the six best orgasms of your life in one night."

"Just six?"

"Six squared?" Warner proposed.

"Mmmm, sounds delish, but you wouldn't scratch me with your claws, would you? I can't have any marks on my body, it's my livelihood."

"Trust me, my lady. You'd be surprised with what I could to your body. What's more, when you fuck a werewolf in transition it gives all-new meaning to the word *shag*."

"Ew. Not that I haven't enjoyed being with you in the past, I just don't think I could handle all the hair."

Warner laughed out loud. Before transformation, he maintained a smooth chest, rippled hard along the planes. Having sex in transaction would keep growth at bay, he assured the faerie. "Better for traction anyway, my love."

"Ah, well. You should have said something earlier." Warner could clearly picture Falona pouting on the other line. "I lined up another gig tonight."

"Cancel it. I'll double your fee for Anton's party."

"Sorry, sweetie. You know what they say. So much cake..." And Falona rang off without a goodbye.

"Bah." So much for having his cake and eating her, too. Calling other women to bide this time was not an option this month. He had promised Anton discretion as far the party was concerned, yet word leaked out around Sierra Glade anyway. Speculation followed him everywhere, and Warner imagined more than a few of Sierra Glade's eligible young gossips would be happy to spread their legs for him...if it meant an opportunity to slip away and look for clues.

Warner snickered. Women like Sugar Pernell, he mused, the queen mother of Sierra Glade gossip. He recalled seeing her at the shop today, but thankfully hadn't detected her while in the kitchen with Andora. Gossip had a specific scent that wasn't very pleasant.

Warner skulked into the house via the gourmet kitchen and left the retrieval of the party cake to the help. Beautiful as it was, he didn't need to be tempted by the many layers and sugar and flour, not with his transformation imminent.

"Lock it in the cooler," he ordered one short gentleman in a crisp black uniform, crooking his neck toward the kitchen's walk-in refrigerator. "I'll be in my rooms the rest of the evening."

The man named Gale nodded, and Warner smiled sadly. His devoted valet knew the measures that needed to be taken. Shortly before the witching—or rather, *wolfing*—hour, Gale would have the rest of the staff dismissed for their safety, and the contents of the pantry moved into Warner's private parlor for the werewolf's consumption. Had Gale the resources to arrange the alternative method of postponing transformation at such short notice, well, Warner would reward Gale to such an extent that he wouldn't need to work for him anymore.

"Will there be anything else, sir?" Gale's staid voice floated behind Warner as he ascended the stairs.

Warner turned back and paused, his hand gripping the rail. Tiny dark hairs that hadn't been there an hour ago grew in tight curls on his knuckles.

"Can you grow a pussy in the next hour?"

Gale's expression remained deadpan. "Pussies, I'm sorry to report, are not in season at this time."

"Same with raises for smart-assed employees. Good night, Gale." Warner trudged up the stairs, shoulders drooped, and dismissed the fleeting notion he entertained of switching teams. He doubted Gale would be *that* willing to serve, raise or no raise.

Chapter Four

Fifteen minutes before the hour, Warner lay shirtless and itching like mad on his bedroom floor. Candy wrappers and potato chip bags, spent and shining with grease, littered the carpet and his clothing. He had eaten—no, inhaled—everything in sight, to no avail. His jaw ached, his cock ached, and as Warner lay perfectly still he could feel the tingling sensation of a billion follicles about to simultaneously explode.

He tested his fangs with his tongue. They had grown in the last hour, and would soon take over his entire mouth, assuming they didn't succumb to cavities from all the crap he'd eaten.

Damn it. The binging hadn't worked. It usually did; what went wrong? It wasn't like he needed to eat things in a particular order. Perhaps it was the growing pull of lustful thoughts, the wondering of what sexual passions could have been enjoyed with Fae Falona, that voided everything he did tonight to curb the wolf.

As Warner crawled across the carpet, his upper body bathed in sweat, he fought to keep a rational mind. The wolf became stronger, poised to take over his being and urge him over the balcony to roam the outskirts of Sierra Glade. He clutched the red velvet drapes dusting the floor, allowing himself only a glance through the slivers of fabric that teased him with shots of the rising moon.

Full...sated, it was, as his appetite should be now. Instead his feet scraped inside designer shoes, close to transforming to spike-nailed paws. His thighs and cock rapidly expanded and contracted, testing the resilience of his slacks. He fumbled with awkward fingers to cast them off before the threatening changes to his body did just that for him, thereby forcing him to throw away a very expensive pair of pants.

He needed to stop the transformation, by any means necessary. Sucking wind through teeth that hadn't yet sharpened, he scuttled out the door on all fours, grimacing as he went. This type of behavior normally indicated that he was past the point of no return. He could only hope Gale was still around, puttering in the kitchen with a sponge and spray can of oven cleaner.

He hoped the valet was indeed bent into the oven, it would save some time. Warner could slam his cock into the Gale's taut little ass and satisfy some of the wolf's desire. Never mind waiting for Gale to undress, either; Warner was certain his cock was hard enough to plow through just about anything. Pants, walls, force fields...

The kitchen was deserted, like the rest of the house. Warner tried his best to nod and hold onto rational thought. Of course, Warner knew Gale to be no fool. The valet no doubt bolted for the front door after delivering Warner's emergency rations. To his credit, he had also left the auxiliary pantry unlocked for Warner to raid.

So he did raid it. Five minutes to the hour saw Warner slouched against the pantry threshold, tearing through a pillow-sized bag of hard pretzels.

Still, it wasn't enough. A normal human, having eaten this much, would likely be vomiting for hours. Warner's enhanced system merely processed everything into an energy that only boosted the wolf...and his sexual desires.

The food slowed, and helped a little, but only a woman could curb the transformation. With minutes to go until the moon reached peak position, the only woman with whom Warner stood a chance was the fake one perched atop Anton's cake.

The cake.

Warner slipped further into the pantry and eyed the stainless steel door of the walk-in refrigerator. The solid green, lighted pinprick indicated that Gale had forgotten to set the lock.

And the wolf, hungry and having all but conquered rational thought, stalked toward the door licking his lips.

* * * * *

Wha – ?

Sugar woke, still naked, shivering, and miserable, curled in a fetal position. By some miracle, she could see the outline of her hands in a faint light—in sleep she couldn't control her invisibility. Her knuckles ached from the cold, and she imagined her skin now bore a bluish tint.

Hopelessness had given way hours ago to fatigue, leading Sugar into a deep slumber. There, freedom — and blood circulation — was just a delicious dream. What she felt now, though, might normally be described the same way, but Sugar felt too out of sorts to be certain. What *was* that scraping against her ass?

She tried to move, but her entire body was numb due to its confined position. She felt close to bodily atrophy, the only sensations breaking through being the chill from the surrounding temperature of the cooler and the twitching ecstasy that accompanied every teasing touch to her sensitive flesh.

Ooh. She tried to cry out, but fatigue had also taken her voice.

She felt a tongue, though. Most definitely a tongue licking the broad curve of her ass...and prodding the cleft in search of her anus. That was a tongue rimming her right now.

"Oh!" came a high-pitched croak as her limbs spasmed in response. One arm shot through the bottom, thickest layer of the cake. She would have expressed some despair at having ruined the cake, but the knowledge that somebody else had torn into it to get to her lifted the guilt.

To say nothing of flooding her pussy. Teeth, tongue, lips...nibbling and licking and kissing her through crumbling cake and frosting. Sugar managed to shift her lower hip and thrust her ass backward to enhance this wonderful dream.

It wasn't a dream, though. Sugar realized as much when she managed to prop her head on her elbow, scraping away more of the cake's inner wall, to see who was spoiling his dinner with dessert. So many people lived and worked at the Doctorow mansion, and she couldn't begin to guess which of them would help her escape by eating...and eating. How would anyone know she was here, anyway?

Light filtered slowly from the open door of the cooler. Sugar squinted to make out the grunting form feasting on her cunt, gasping at first sight of Warner's unmistakable profile, shadowed in the foreground.

Warner. Had he detected her scent?

Sugar felt her heart slide to the cake floor. Warner lifted his head momentarily to catch his breath, and Sugar noticed his brows were thicker, and his mane of dark hair unruly and coarse. Was tonight a full moon? The *Snitch* reported the lunar calendar. Sugar sighed. She really needed to read that rag for other things besides her byline.

One thing she *did* know, without having to read the paper, was that sex with a werewolf in transition could be quite exhilarating. She'd dated a werewolf in college. Fortuitous, it would have to be, for the cake to be here. They'd need the extra energy.

Slowly, with every broad stroke against her anus, then up her pussy lips to her clit, life sparked throughout her body. She quivered and twisted her body, easing slightly onto her back and parting her knees as wide as possible. Warner had eaten away a large enough hole to allow her to stretch her legs forward, and she brought her heels together behind Warner's neck.

He seemed not to notice, but was lost in his own little world, teasing her pussy lips and clit with rapid oral prodding.

That's it. Sugar moaned softly. More where that came from. Sweets for the sweet.

Above them, the rest of the cake teetered to the point of collapse, but Sugar didn't care. Let it avalanche.

The fervor with which she welcomed her orgasm was all that was needed to encourage the cake to topple. The remaining, intact layers fell noiselessly to the floor around them. Cracked sugar frosting flakes and marzipan ribbons rained gently down, covering them like new fallen snow.

No matter. Warner would lick her body clean, and she would return the favor, she decided as Warner doused her fading fires with broad swipes up her pussy lips.

When instead he leaned back with a sticky, satisfied grin, Sugar gasped. The cock that sprang forward, its tip shining with pre-cum, was the largest she had even seen. Yes, she would return the favor, assuming she survived.

"Warner." Her voice was still small and barely audible in the dim, yet gained profound strength as Warner launched forward, punching holes into the bottom cake layer with his fists for support. Cradled between her parted thighs, Warner shifted his hips upward and rolled his cock over her quivering flesh. He teased her slick core and sensitive inner labia, then thrust upward and scraped her clit with the bulging head of his cock. Sugar was powerless to move, as Warner's upper body pressed against hers. She managed to squirm a bit, synchronized to his touch, feeling dizzy from each gust of warm breath tickling her breasts and setting her nipples to peak.

"You bastard," she groaned, and arched her neck upward to meet a pair of dripping fangs that lightly skimmed twin lines down her throat. She meant it, of course, in the nicest possible sense of the word.

"Yummy," was the werewolf's response, and he thrust his cock into her waiting pussy unaided.

* * * * *

Conscious thought returned in full the second Warner entered her. He felt the wolf's grasp on his mind slide away as Sugar's pussy clamped around his cock. Tightened muscles pulled him deeper inside her, and rapid, urgent thrusts smoothed into a steadier rhythm that he could enjoy as well.

"So yummy." Mashed, moist cake oozed between his fingers as he fisted his hands, and he smeared the result over Sugar's smooth, flat belly. Mingled with her own unique taste, Andora's recipe could only be improved.

He had an idea of how Sugar got into his house. She had been hiding in the cake! Somehow, she eluded him at Sweet Surprise and slipped inside the cake as he paid for it. She knew of the spell and triggered it, and his keen sense of smell hadn't detected her. Then he remembered he'd *heard* something.

The bitch. The sneaky, deliciously tight bitch.

She nearly scared Warner to death when he tucked into the bottom layer of the cake and hit skin on the third bite. Briefly, in his wolf-addled mind, there had been the thought to howl his displeasure at the breach of security, but a few seconds of rimming Sugar's beautiful rounded ass convinced the wolf that he had no reason to be displeasured. She tasted sweeter than anything on Sweet Surprise's menu.

A mouth full of pussy, too, trumped a mouth voicing displeasure any day. And Sugar's pussy was the perfect tonic to quelling his anger over her presence in his home...and the cake's destruction. That he couldn't blame on her, of course, but once the euphoria of this fuck subsided he was going to have to take issue with her being here.

First, he closed his eyes and focused on his cock, memorizing every ridge and curve within her tight vaginal walls that kept his cock hard and ready to come. When he did, he thought he could go on forever. He could swear his cry rattled the jars on the surrounding shelves.

His cock was still hard when he pulled out; sugar frosting and cake crumbs clung to his shaft as he rubbed away the ache. "Come here," he ordered a limp Sugar, and grasped her by the waist. "Take me in your mouth."

Sugar complied quickly. The dimmed light might have been a hindrance for the lovely reporter, but Warner's keen wolfish eyesight allowed him perfect night vision. It wasn't difficult, therefore, to detect the sly grin on Sugar's face or the glint in her bright eyes as her face lowered toward his cock.

Grasping him at the base of his shaft, Sugar licked him clean. She kissed away crumbs and rolled his aching head in her mouth, working his shaft as one would a Popsicle. Given his good vision, though, even he couldn't tell where his cum ended and the cake began.

"You like that, babe?" he moaned.

"Mmm." Sugar smacked her lips and pressed them to his throbbing head. "Sorry about the cake."

The cake. Warner sighed. Five thousand dollars, *poof*. Still, it wasn't the most expensive fuck he'd enjoyed. "No matter," he sighed. "Anton had no idea what to expect, so no harm done. I'll think of an alternative, ah, snack.

"You," he continued, taking Sugar by the back the neck and lifting her to meet his eyes, "will also have no idea what to expect."

Chapter Five

The heavy door leading back into the pantry opened further on its own, and now Sugar could see clearly the wicked gleam in Warner's eyes. She didn't feel so comfortable with this hungry look, one that implied he would chew her up and spit her out in another sense.

She doubted she'd enjoy that as much. She tried to ease away from Warner's grasp but his hold remained steadfast.

"Warner," she said, the tremor in her voice evident, "let me explain."

"Explain? What, you took a wrong turn leaving the ice cream shop and ended up in my cake by accident, thinking it was your car?" He clucked at her. "Granted, I've seen that matchbox you drive, and given your sloppiness in reporting of late I can understand how you might be confused."

"I got by you, didn't I?" she snapped.

Warner said nothing, only snorted his displeasure. Sugar noticed how quickly his wolf-coarse hair and eyebrows had receded as he shook his head at her. Primitive desire, however he tried to mask it behind his anger, was still there.

"Besides," she said, irritated, "if not for me you'd have wolfed out completely, or whatever it is you call it. I know that can't be good the night before Anton's party. So, I did you a favor, whether you want to admit it or not."

"You did, and I thank you, my dear," Warner conceded with a slight grin. Easing off of her, he brushed away what flakes of frosting and marizpan still clung to his marvelously chiseled body. His cock still stood high. Sugar closed her thighs together to quell the soreness that resulted after their coupling, and hoped Warner wouldn't take the gesture as refusal of another round.

"Normally I'd have you upstairs so fast you'd wonder how we got there without moving," he was saying as he helped her stand. Sugar was conscious of his gaze inspecting her every curve; she was sticky with marzipan and sugar paste. "As it is, my dear, I appear sated enough not to have to worry about changing tonight. I can't have you here in the morning when the caterers and planners arrive, either. So, you'll have to do me the favor of leaving."

He guided her out of the cooler, through the pantry to the kitchen. Sugar marveled at its expanse and technological majesty. It put the kitchen of Sweet Surprise to shame. The rest of Warner's mansion was certainly no less opulent, she imagined. She had to wonder where the main event would take place.

She had to *know*. She had to stay and see it for herself, and get it on paper for Melina.

Warner reached for a wall phone. "Gale isn't far. I'll have him get the car and drive you home," he said."

"If you insist," Sugar said. She toed a circle on the marble tile floor. "But you'll have to do something for me first."

Warner looked up from dialing Gale's number. "That is?"

Sugar smiled. "Catch me."

*****

Just like that, she faded into the air with a light giggle. The sound of bare feet skidding against the kitchen floor signaled her hasty escape.

Warner disconnected before Gale could answer. "I can still see cake sticking to you," he called after her. "You won't be that difficult to find."

"Catch me if you can, wolf boy." Sugar's voice was distant now, taunting and mirthful. Warner looked down at the kitchen floor, streaked with frosting prints. No, she wouldn't be difficult to find at all. Andora's magnetism may have distracted him enough not to detect Sugar at the ice cream parlor, but here her unique scent would take prominence over more familiar surroundings. How silly to run from a werewolf; Warner would sniff her out in no time.

Then, he mused silently, she'd do him the favor of...doing him.

*****

She managed to get as much of the cake off her body as possible. Her skin still felt sticky and uncomfortable, but a chance turn down a long hallway led her to a guest bathroom. There she wet a rag and swabbed her limbs, breasts, and backside, before slipping quietly back to the main foyer. She had to find a good place to hide; more than likely she wouldn't make it long, but she wanted to give Warner a good chase.

Though she enjoyed the chase, she wanted to be caught. Warner only seemed angry with her for running, she knew. She relished the punishment to ensue from this chase as much, if not more, than chasing the story for the *Snitch*.

Once in the foyer, she ascended the main staircase slowly, so as not to creak on any steps. A cursory search of the main floor yielded no doors leading to a basement, leading Sugar to guess Warner had no basement rec room. Sugar could only guess that the party would encompass much of the house rather than be limited to one room, with the main event taking place in one of the bedrooms.

The main event, certainly, would involve the lovely Fae Falona, but who else? Warner? The groom? Both? The notion disturbed Sugar, and as images of Warner bent over Fae Falona surfaced she felt all the more unnerved.

Sugar shook the thoughts away. *Come on*, the reporter inside her urged. The sex was fun, but she wasn't Warner's girl.

Whom was she kidding? The sex was more than fun. The sex was better than cake, tastier than even Andora's majestic tribute to matrimonial pastry.

She hurried down the hall. A man, a werewolf, obsessed with appearances like Warner no doubt had living quarters suited to his libido. If Warner were astute enough to track her down, fine, but she wanted to at least see his living quarters once. Despite how much Warner appeared to enjoy their coupling, she doubted she'd ever receive a formal invitation. And, if she had to be caught, she could think of no better place.

She checked every door, looking constantly over her shoulder and listening for Warner's heavy, wolfish panting. It wasn't long before Sugar found the correct entrance, and her suspicions of Warner's tastes were confirmed as she stepped carefully across the lush carpet into a bedroom fit for a film star. On the far end, an open balcony door exposed through the curtains a twinkling Sierra Glade, her lights alive like distant fireflies and fairies against the inky black.

The bureau and dresser were ominous, nearly taking up one wall with an impressive mirror that seemed more like a portal into an alternative universe. Of course, given the nature of Sierra Glade, it could be one.

Befitting of a man with impeccable taste in wardrobe, Sugar decided. Certainly, Warner wouldn't wear the same pair of underwear twice; he probably had a year's supply of briefs folded neatly in these drawers. Assuming, Sugar realized with a smirk, the werewolf wore underwear at all.

The bed stood huge, draped in ivory sheets so smooth Sugar imagined a headfirst dive would feel like falling into a vat of milk. The bed lay positioned in the middle of the large room atop a platform, Sugar guessed, to emphasize the importance of Warner's sexual prowess. Mahogany bookshelves lined the wall supporting it; Sugar silently ticked off titles of numerous classics and spell books. Who knew that Warner was so literate? She noticed bends and wrinkles in the covers and pages...these books weren't for show.

"Interested in borrowing something? Perhaps you see something else in the room that suits your fancy."

She started at the sound of Warner's bemusement, and on instinct checked her arms. She saw nothing, therefore Warner shouldn't have, either. Had she inadvertently read aloud a book title without realizing it, or maybe he could hear her breathing?

"I know you're here, Sugar," Warner said, his voice as smooth as the sheets she now gazed at with longing. The husky tone of each spoken word chilled her, while her nipples stood to attention and her pussy ached for that mouth. Her toes curled into the carpet, and she didn't doubt she could pull up some of the shag fibers.

Shag. Remembering the earlier confrontation with Melina, she glanced down at the carpet. Two deep indentations in the shag marked where she stood, and though the room was dimly lit she was certain Warner's wolfish eyesight caught it right off the bat. *Damn it.*

"I followed the wet spots," Warner continued, drawing closer. Sugar felt the heat of his desire resonate and envelop her, stoking the fire smoldering in her pussy. "A bit of advice, Sugar, when you hose yourself down—or whatever it was you did to get the cake crumbs off—it helps to dry yourself before you take off running."

Sugar remained still. He was practically on top of her now, presumably using her footprints as a guide. She flinched when a hand brushed her backside. From her point of view, Warner appeared to make odd hand gestures, sizing up a woman's shape. Her shape.

"I followed the wet spots, through the foyer, up the stairs and down the hall. Naturally, I assumed water, but I have to wonder what else is wet." Warner sized up the space she filled and waved his hands until he touched skin. Sugar let out a pleasured gasp - no point in remaining quiet - and willed herself to be seen.

"Now that's cheating," Warner admonished, turning his head. "Have you fucked anyone while invisible?"

"No," Sugar said. Odd that she hadn't, she surmised. Then again, there hadn't been many men in her life, nor many men she wanted to fuck. Now, she thought only of the one standing before her.

Moved by Warner's piercing gaze, she rendered herself invisible again. He palmed her belly. "Much better. I know what this is, so if I move down..."

Slowly his fingers danced down her quivering abdomen into the valley that concealed her slick core. "So this is what an invisible pussy feels like," he chuckled. "Does it feel any different invisible?"

Words failed Sugar. The sensation flooding her pussy and shooting through her veins felt ten times better than any touch, kiss, or caress she'd ever enjoyed. This mere dabbling of her pussy lips as Warner explored her, surpassed nearly everything he had done to her in the cooler. She wobbled in place, certain her legs would give out if he continued.

"And this," he said, delving a finger deeper into her labial folds, "must be..."

Sugar cried aloud. The touch to her clit set off fireworks. Record time for an orgasm...now *that* was an exclusive the *Snitch* would never print.

"It must." Warner tested his hands and soon had Sugar's unseen body in his arms. Sugar felt herself lifted high as he carried her toward the bed. The room became a blur. The arousal she experienced now seemed magnified by her invisibility, as if her skin were stripped to leave Warner to sample a more sensitive body.

She could only hope, she decided as he lay her gently against the top sheet, that he'd have no trouble finding the right hole with that thickening cock. Warner lay on top of her, rubbing his cock against her thighs, belly, and cunt, in search of that secret cove. It felt good, and given this enhanced state, she could only imagine how his cock would feel inside her.

"Little help here, darlin'?" Warner rocked his hips from side to side, parting her legs enough to allow the tip of his cock to tap against her parted pussy lips. Sugar breathed slowly, feeling her chest expand and thrilled by the fact that she couldn't be seen. That Warner appeared to be humping the bed might have looked amusing to anybody else, but Sugar found the primal stretching of his body, his muscular arms braced on either side of her, very erotic. He appeared to hover, but she felt his heat as they touched, and as Warner slowly entered her...oh!

"Incredible," he said on a sigh. "I'm fucking you, I'm fucking you while you're invisible. I can actually see my cock...and you're so damn tight."

"You're so thick." *Wonderfully thick.* Cake frosting should be so thick. It could stand up on its own.

She tilted her head back to accept Warner's kisses. For the most part he was on target, and she had to giggle every time his head dipped low and missed. Sugar could only imagine, too, what kissing her while invisible must have looked like from his point of view. As it was, watching his hips pivot as he slammed his cock into her pussy was a sight that would never bore her.

When his orgasm neared, he slid out quickly and came on her belly, making patches of skin visible with his seed. That soon disappeared as his body crushed against hers for one last kiss.

"Come out, come out, wherever you are," he sang. "Rather, just come."

In seconds, Sugar was visible again, and eager to respond as Warner pulled back the sheets to guide her into bed. "I thought I was going home," she challenged him, her tone light.

Warner pulled the sheets over them and drew Sugar close, easing her to her side and spooning her. "You are, in the morning," he said. "Right now, I'm going to need your help."

"Really? What good could a soon-to-be out of work reporter be to you?" No way was Melina keeping her at the *Snitch* after this. Her job was to report gossip, not personify it. Sugar had no doubt word of this would spread.

In fact...Sugar tilted her head toward the open window. She could have sworn she saw something tiny fluttering against the curtains, tiny like a nosy fairy reporter's wings.

Let him watch, she thought, if Winkle was indeed out there.

"I can think of one thing." Warner said as he nipped her ear, eliciting a giggle from Sugar. "Before we get to that, however, I'm going to need some ideas on an alternate party plan for Anton. With the cake destroyed, most of the party's agenda goes with it."

Sugar closed her eyes and focused on Warner's hands exploring her length. She was thinking of a number of things herself, nothing to do with Anton's bachelor party. "Too bad, for Anton, anyway," she said. "But won't he be disappointed if you change plans?"

"Probably not," Warner said. "In truth, he's probably the least enthusiastic about the party. He'd be happy with a group outing at Sweet Surprise, splitting one of those ice cream boats instead of getting a lap dance. He's in love with his fiancée, you know."

"Good to know, considering he's about to commit to her for the rest of his life," Sugar said. Good to know, too, Warner seemed less and less disappointed himself that the party, and the lovely Fae Falona's performance, wouldn't happen.

Then, she said, "What are you doing?" She smiled as he leered at her.

Warner slid a hand over her hip and between her legs. "Me? Oh, I'm just ready for a midnight snack."

Sugar eased onto her back as Warner moved over her. "Is the wolf in you ever satisfied?"

"For your sake, darling," Warner said, brushing his lips against hers, "you better hope not."

About the Author

Leigh Ellwood writes spicy romances and sassy mysteries. She is the creator of the award-winning Dareville series for Phaze Books and DLP Books, as well as numerous shorts for other small publishers. Readers are invited to visit her website for more information on Leigh's books.

http://www.leighellwood.com
http://leighwantsfood.blogspot.com
http://twitter.com/LeighEllwood

Also by Leigh Ellwood

In the Dareville series…

Truth or Dare
The Dares That Bind
Dare Me
Daring Young Man
Double Dare
Dare to Dream
Dare and Dare Alike
Daringly Delicious
A Winter's Dare
By the Chimney With Dare
Handle With Dare
Where Angels Dare to Tread
Dare to Act

Also available…

Jilted
Surveillance
Why, Why, Zed?
M-Squared
She Loves Me
Enter Sandman
Midnight Passions

and many more…

Made in the USA
Charleston, SC
18 November 2012